7

DO YOU
LOVE YOUR
MOM
and Her TWO-Hit
Multi-Target
Attacks
?

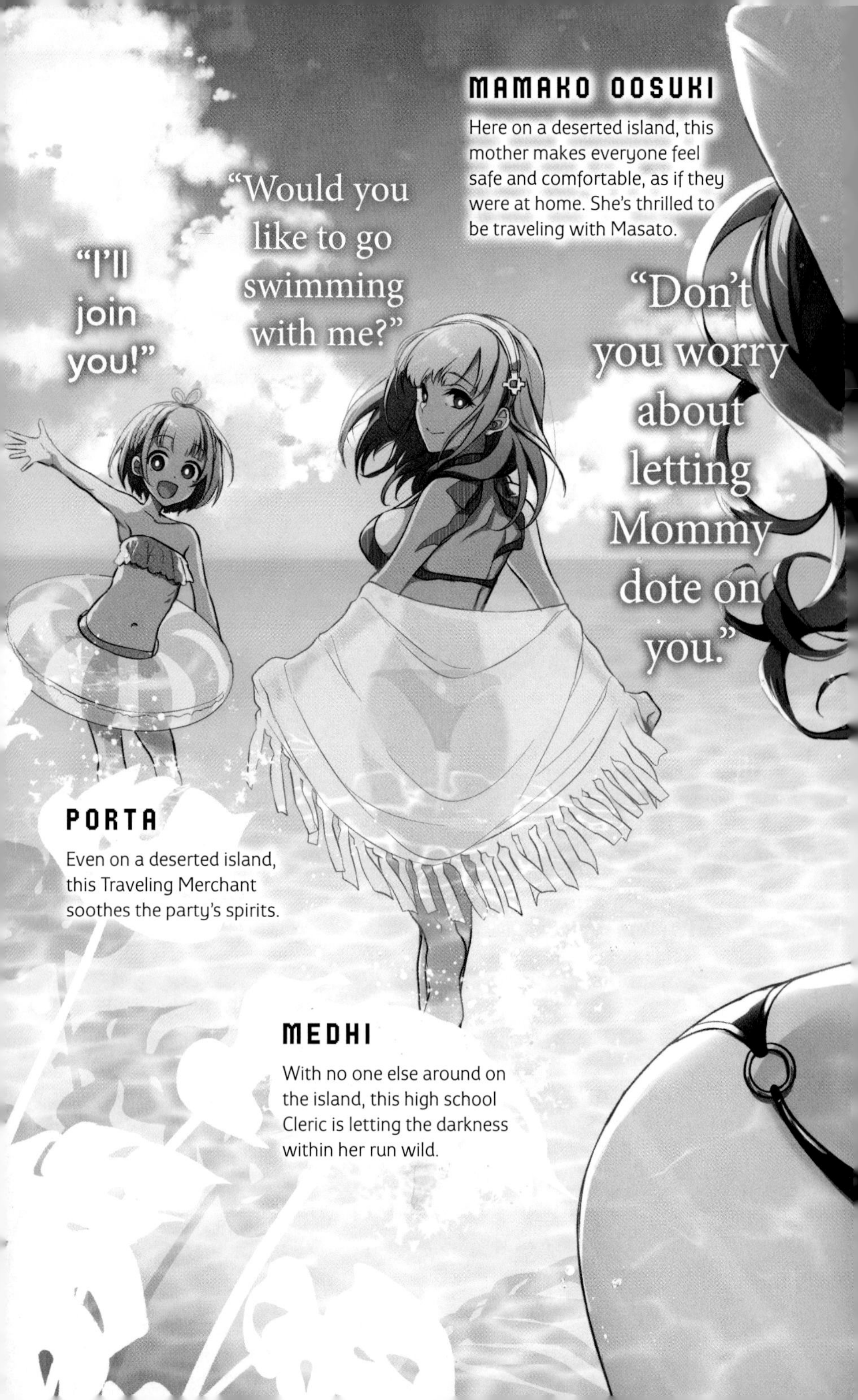
MAMAKO OOSUKI
Here on a deserted island, this mother makes everyone feel safe and comfortable, as if they were at home. She's thrilled to be traveling with Masato.
"Don't you worry about letting Mommy dote on you."
"Would you like to go swimming with me?"
"I'll join you!"
PORTA
Even on a deserted island, this Traveling Merchant soothes the party's spirits.
MEDHI
With no one else around on the island, this high school Cleric is letting the darkness within her run wild.

"This is the resort we dreamed of!"

WISE

You'd think there'd be no way she could get her magic sealed on an uninhabited island, yet this high school Sage found a way.

"Mamako Oosuki ain't no threat to Frighten-Mom Fratello!"

FRATELLO

Another of the Four Heavenly Kings of the Libere Rebellion. A Fighter prone to emphasizing his masculinity.

"You women are so stupid and incompetent… It makes me want to puke."

"Ack…"

"Urrrrgh…"

AMANTE

Another of the Four Heavenly Kings of the Libere Rebellion. A pitiful Magic Fencer prone to blabbing important information.

SORELLA

One of the Four Heavenly Kings of the Libere Rebellion. A pitiful Necromancer whose schemes never work out.

The Legend of Ma-kun Quiz

"If you get all of these right, that makes you Ma-kun's mommy!"

Q1: Okay, first question! How old was Ma-kun when he first stood up all by himself?

Q2: What did Ma-kun like to do at home when he was little?

Q3: Do you know what Ma-kun's favorite foods are?

Q4: When did Ma-kun first display a special power?

Q5: Bonus question! When did Ma-kun set out on his adventure?

A1: He was seven months old! He just stood straight up and stared right at Mommy! Already acting like a hero!

A2: He drew pictures of Mommy... No, those must have been sigils! By giving them to Mommy, he increased my parental power!

A3: Ma-kun's never been a picky eater, but he does like meat the best. Maybe that's why his endurance and attack have gotten so high!

A4: He was in his second year of junior high. I heard him laughing in his room and shouting something about fire and ice!

A5: His first year of high school! Ma-kun had grown so big, and he set off to unknown realms...of course, with his mommy! Hee-hee!

Quit trying to turn mundane stuff into legends. And *please* stop revealing all my embarrassing secrets!

CONTENTS

Dachima Inaka

Do you love your MOM and Her Two-Hit Multi-Target Attacks?

VOLUME 7

DACHIMA INAKA

Illustration by IIDA POCHI.

YEN ON
New York

Do You Love Your Mom and Her Two-Hit Multi-Target Attacks?, Vol. 7

▶ Dachima Inaka

▶ Translation by Andrew Cunningham

▶ Cover art by Iida Pochi.

This book is a work of fiction. Names, characters, places, and incidents are the product of the author's imagination or are used fictitiously. Any resemblance to actual events, locales, or persons, living or dead, is coincidental.

TSUJO KOGEKI GA ZENTAI KOGEKI DE 2KAI KOGEKI NO OKASAN WA SUKI DESUKA? Vol. 7
©Dachima Inaka, Iida Pochi. (2018)
First published in Japan in 2018 by KADOKAWA CORPORATION, Tokyo.
English translation rights arranged with KADOKAWA CORPORATION, Tokyo, through TUTTLE-MORI AGENCY, INC., Tokyo.

English translation © 2020 by Yen Press, LLC

First Yen On Edition: November 2020

Yen On is an imprint of Yen Press, LLC.
The Yen On name and logo are trademarks of Yen Press, LLC.

The publisher is not responsible for websites (or their content) that are not owned by the publisher.

▶ Yen On
150 West 30th Street, 19th Floor
New York, NY 10001

▶ Visit us at yenpress.com
facebook.com/yenpress
twitter.com/yenpress
yenpress.tumblr.com
instagram.com/yenpress

Library of Congress Cataloging-in-Publication Data
Names: Inaka, Dachima, author. | Pochi., Iida, illustrator. | Cunningham, Andrew, 1979– translator.
Title: Do you love your mom and her two-hit multi-target attacks? / Dachima Inaka ; illustration by Iida Pochi. ; translation by Andrew Cunningham.
Other titles: Tsujo kogeki ga zentai kogeki de 2kai kogeki no okasan wa suki desuka?. English
Description: First Yen On edition. | New York : Yen On, 2018–
Identifiers: LCCN 2018030739 | ISBN 9781975328009 (v. 1 : pbk.) | ISBN 9781975328375 (v. 2 : pbk.) | ISBN 9781975328399 (v. 3 : pbk.) | ISBN 9781975328412 (v. 4 : pbk.) | ISBN 9781975359423 (v. 5 : pbk.) | ISBN 9781975359430 (v. 6 : pbk.) | ISBN 9781975306311 (v. 7 : pbk.)
Subjects: LCSH: Virtual reality—Fiction.
Classification: LCC PL871.5.N35 T7813 2018 | DDC 895.63/6—dc23
LC record available at https://lccn.loc.gov/2018030739

ISBNs: 978-1-9753-0631-1 (paperback)
        978-1-9753-0951-0 (ebook)

10 9 8 7 6 5 4 3 2 1

LSC-C

Printed in the United States of America

Prologue　To All MMMMMMORPG (Working Title)
Test Players

Thank you all for your cooperation with our beta testing.

We have some important news for you all.

A new area has been added!

For this game, it was always our intention to provide a vast and varied world by connecting the main ministry server to local servers run by the forty-seven prefectural governments.

Until now, only the main Tokyo server has been online, but the Aichi server has finally reached the testing phase, so the area hosted on that server is now available to test players!

The name of this new world is: Materland.

Aichi Prefecture is perhaps best known for the Higashiyama Zoo and Botanical Gardens, boasting the most species of any zoo in Japan! What world will Aichi bring us?

That's up to you test players to find out!

To celebrate the grand opening, Materland is holding a special event where they're giving away items that should prove useful on your adventures.

A lucky few may receive extra-special prizes not obtainable anywhere else!

We're looking forward to your visit!

*How to Access

1. From the transfer point near the Catharn capital, make your way to the Transport Palace.

2. In the Transport Palace area, move to the island labeled Materland.

3. Stand on the magic circle to be transferred! (Delays may occur in the interest of safety.)

*Precautions
Some sections of Materland are being used for a special admin investigation, so only areas accessible by test players will be reflected in your map data.
Please refrain from accessing areas outside of that range.

"...It's not like it's been that long since I was last here, but it sure feels like it," Masato said as he and his party waited on the magic circle that would take them to Materland.

Battling his impatience, he tried to take in the view.

Stretching as far as the eye could see were floating islands connected by hanging bridges.

It was an unreal sight, but he had seen it before; this was the Transport Palace area—The first place Masato had seen when he entered the game.

On the biggest island was the resplendent Transport Palace itself—and on the veranda stood the king.

He was staring at Masato, looking very sad—like, about-to-burst-into-tears sad.

"Erm...uh...maybe we should've stopped by and said hi at some point..."

Feeling guilty, Masato avoided the king's gaze.

But Wise and Medhi kept staring back at the king.

"Whatever. That king's only here for the initial tutorial."

"Once we've obtained the special bonus starting equipment, we have no further use for him."

"Well, this *is* a game, so you have a point, but...you could be nicer about it. I mean, look!"

Had the king heard them? He'd covered his face with his hands, slumping over. He looked really depressed.

But never fear! Porta, the living embodiment of good cheer, was here with them!

"When we're in Materland, I'm going to buy a souvenir for the king! We can give it to him the next time we see him! Just you wait!"

Porta waved at him, and the king jumped to his feet and happily waved back. At least he had recovered quickly.

But as this was going on, the circle beneath their feet began to glow.

"Here we go! Nobody forgot anything, right?"

"Well, maybe Mone? But we can't exactly leave the Mom Shop unattended."

"That shop is an important consultation center for poor lost souls. And Mone herself said she'd rather focus on her work there, so we should leave her to it."

"I'll buy a souvenir for Mone, too! I'll buy lots of souvenirs!"

"Right. Well, with that settled—"

"Hold on. We haven't finished making sure Masato has everything," Wise interrupted, grinning. Medhi and Porta seemed to be enjoying this, too.

That spelled trouble.

"Let's run through this before we get transported. Masato, got your weapon?"

"Yep. Right here."

"All your armor?" asked Medhi.

"Uh-huh. All equipped."

"Masato! Do you have your recovery items— Oh, I have those!"

"We leave all of that to you, Porta! Which means—"

"Then last up! Mommy!"

Mamako slid up next to Masato and locked elbows, pressing his arm into her.

Party. Weapons. Armor. Items. And Mommy.

Everything you need for an adventure!

"……Siiiiiiiiiiiiiigh…………"

"O-oh my? What's wrong, Ma-kun? Such a dramatic sigh! D-don't you want to be with Mommy?"

"No, that's not it…"

Maybe being here again had brought it all back.

He'd been thrown into a game and had thought he was starting a grand solo adventure...only to have his mother come running after him, leading to a big blowout.

And then he'd spent a lot of time trying to somehow get stronger than her, to no avail.

And now?

"I'm just shaking my head at myself. Like, I'm *so* over complaining about you being here... I've improved myself, just not the way I planned to."

He glanced at the Transport Palace again and saw the king giving him an approving nod.

He'd achieved the results expected of a Normal Hero.

Part of him was still not happy about that, but...whatever.

"Our goal is to tour this new area and obtain the exclusive event items. Let's do this!"

"Ma-kun and Mommy will have even more adventures there!"

"Yeah, yeah, we'll adventure together. Just leggo of my arm!"

Saying these things had no effect, though. She just smiled happily, her grip not loosening at all. As he was bathed in the warm smiles of his party, the light of the transport spell enveloped them.

What was waiting for them on the other side? Well...

Chapter 1   So Begins the Harshest, Yet Most Tragically Overprotected Adventure in History.

The newly opened world, Materland. A natural paradise.

Or perhaps "vegetable paradise" would be more accurate.

The ground was covered not in green grass but in green onions. Truly massive potatoes formed a sort of rocky zone. Beyond that was an edible forest of giant broccoli.

"Yikes…that's a lotta veggies," said Wise.

"It certainly is," agreed Medhi.

"Nothing but veggies!" added Porta.

"Yep. I don't know what else to say, really…"

"Hee-hee! It's like we're tiny and wandered into a field! And we can do all the cooking we like!"

"Yeah, this seemed like a world for you, Mom. Anyway, if we end up eating well, I ain't complaining. Should we get moving?"

They took a spiral staircase made of snow peas down from the transport point and headed for the nearest settlement.

No gates or walls, just an open layout…and once again, a series of impressed noises from the party.

"So, this is Materland's first location, Materville… Wow. It's, uh… very naturalistic."

It was at least as big as Catharn's capital, yet somehow the *ville* part still felt right.

None of the buildings were made of bricks or earthen walls. The homes were made out of giant hollowed-out produce or located inside naturally occurring crevices. Some of the houses even looked like birds' nests resting on giant broccoli stalks.

The rivers and roads were of simple make, with only enough work done to make them passable. Everything else was left as nature intended: a wild world, living in harmony with the elements.

"This is definitely on the fantastical end of fantasy," said Wise.

"Like something out of a fairy tale…," said Medhi. "Also…"

"…Those must be the inhabitants," added Masato.

As the party entered town, pointy ears twitched, tails swished, wings rustled, and all eyes turned toward them.

There were cat ears, dog and reptilian tails, bird and bat wings—of all shapes and patterns, but with each part being extremely distinctive.

What do we call it when animal parts grow from a human body?

"Wow! Beastkin!" squealed Porta. "All kinds of beastkin!!"

"So this is a beastkin world. Oh, they have merfolk, too."

A beautiful green-scaled mermaid had poked her face out of the water. "H-hi…," Masato said with a slight nod of his head. "Hiii!" she replied, waving back. A small moment, but one that made him very happy.

A world of natural beauty…and animal ears.

Materland.

This place is awesome!

Masato was overjoyed. What a wonderful world this was!

Then…

"Ma-kun, I know you're busy flirting with that mermaid, but do you have a moment?"

"What is it with moms and reading everything the wrong way? I'm not flirting with her! …So? What is it, Mom?"

"There seem to be an awful lot of beastkin gathering around us. Is that bad?"

"Huh? *Gathering*…?"

He looked around, and indeed, they'd drawn quite a crowd.

On the roads, on the roofs, in the sky above. Easily over a hundred beastkin, all staring right at them.

"Wow, some even have ASCII faces… Aichi's character design department is behind schedule, too. But maybe that's not the most pressing issue here… Um, can I help you all with something?"

Masato was almost afraid to ask.

Every single one of the beastkin grinned.

* * *

"""""Fresh meeeat!"""""

"...Uh?"

Every beastkin had far greater physical capabilities than your average human...and they were all attacking.

The party stood there dumbfounded before being hoisted into the air and carried away.

"""""Heave, ho! Heave, ho!"""""

"W-wait!" shouted Wise. "What the heck? *Fresh meat*?! What are you even talking about?!"

"Does this mean we're going to get eaten?!" wailed Medhi.

"Ohhh, I think you might be right!" said Masato. "There are gonna be some spits over an open fire and we'll be slowly turned above it!"

"Or maybe a big bubbling pot for us to get boiled in!" added Porta.

"I think that would cook us much more evenly. Much less risk of the meat getting burned!"

"Yep, Mom's the expert chef here...but *how* we're gonna get cooked isn't the problem, is it?!"

"I really, really don't want to get eaten! Masato! Masatoooo!"

"I hear a cry for help! But I need rescuing myself! Right, uh...maybe it's time for me to get all heroic and...!"

But before he could start slashing his way out of this crisis...

The crowd stopped and carefully put all five party members down.

They were in a clearing in the center of town, one large enough for a ball game.

No firepits or giant cauldrons, just a sign reading WELCOME TO MATERLAND! It was clearly handmade.

"Um...huh? What's going on?"

"Woo! Surprise!"

The beastkin around them all fired off party poppers.

A cat boy in festival garb came running up amid the flurry of confetti.

"Welcome to Materland! Welcome, everyone!"

"Uh...weren't you going to eat us?"

"That was just our little surprise! Sometimes we get people who think beastkin really eat humans, so we put on a little production to clear up that misunderstanding!"

"...That, uh, seriously scared us."

"Well, you're welcome here, so no need to be scared! Smile, everyone! Smile!"

The cat boy grinned, purring at them.

Grinning back, Masato pulled the cat's whiskers.

"Smile." "I'm sorry! I'm sorry!"

As a reminder, please do not do this to a real cat. Really obnoxious cat boys are fair game, however.

After recovering somewhat...

"So we may have overdone it a bit, but it's all water under the bridge! Welcome to Materland! We're thrilled to have you here!"

"Thanks..."

"Moving right along, as part of our welcome, we'd like to start the event where you'll earn a fabulous prize! Yay!"

"'Kay, let's get this over with."

"We'll get what we came for and then go sightseeing."

"Now, now, ladies. We can't have you taking this event lightly! Materland is a world built around survival of the fittest—if you aren't strong, you won't get anything. And with that said...!"

The cat boy snapped his fingers.

A giant magic circle appeared on the ground beneath them, glowing. Some...*things* began crawling out of it...

"What the...?!"

"Monsters prepared just for this event! Extremely violent, dangerous monsters you would never come across in a normal encounter! And now! Any moment now! They will reveal themselves...!"

"Oh my! Dangerous monsters? We can't have that. *Hyah!*"

Before he could finish the dramatic buildup, Mamako attacked.

The Holy Sword of Earth, Terra di Madre, caused rock spikes to shoot out of the ground!

The Holy Sword of the Ocean, Altura, fired a volley of water bullets!

Just as the monsters were about to appear, they and the magic circle were sliced and stabbed and skewered and eliminated! Combat complete!

"And there you have it."

"Er, um…well…I was still explaining… We had a whole presentation…"

The boy's cat eyes were frozen wide open.

The beastkin around them had been hauling out instruments and tribal drums, preparing to score the battle, and they all froze, too. They were too late!

"Sorry, cat dude. My mom just rolls like that. Seriously, can't apologize enough."

"Hee-hee! I did it! …Oh? What's this?"

A glittering golden ticket appeared in front of Mamako, fluttering down from the sky.

"Cat dude, explain."

"Uh, right… That ticket is the reward for clearing the event! It allows you to use a special gacha and get a prize."

"What, we don't just get the prize directly? Geez, online games these days…so? We only get one ticket for the whole party?"

"No, one for each party member. Yes, that's right… The event isn't over yet! Okay!"

The cat recovered, snapping his fingers.

This time a single magic circle appeared right in front of them. There were no signs of anything emerging from it; instead the pattern just rotated steadily, like a clock marking time.

"Heh-heh-heh…this is a very special magic circle! Any moment now, it'll explode!"

"E-explode?!"

"To stop it, you have to pour enough magic power into it to overwhelm the effect! But that's not possible for any normal mage! Well, what now? You're in grave dan—"

"Humph, this calls for the ultimate Sage!"

Wise took a few steps forward, slapped her hand on the circle, and grunted. MP poured out of her and into the circle.

10 MP…50…100…150…200…300…

The circle stopped rotating! Operation complete!

"W-well? I cleared it! That was actually pretty easy," she panted.

"That was easy?!"

"You're acting like it wasn't a big deal, but you look half-dead...and when did your MP pool get that huge, Wise? Color me surprised."

"Look, I've been leveling up like everyone else! ...And now I get a ticket."

She snatched the ticket out of the air in front of her, grinning proudly.

The crowd, this time fully prepared, played a quick fanfare to celebrate her feat. They seemed pretty pleased with themselves.

Only the cat boy was grinding his teeth in frustration.

"Not just once, but twice?! These aren't supposed to be easy! Hnggg!"

"So much for *welcome*."

"Fine! Be that way! ...Next!"

The cat beastkin snapped his fingers.

This time the circle and pattern were separated. A broken magic circle!

"This is the magic of life, destroyed by a demon lord! If you don't heal it with the right spell, the world itself will be des—"

"Heal? Then it's time for a Healer. You're up, Medhi."

"Yes, this is a Cleric's job... *Spara la magia per mirare... Cura! Alto Cura! Pieno Cura!*"

"I'm not done explaining!"

Without even glancing at the cat, Medhi just kept using magic. The broken circle was covered in a healing light.

The HP assigned to the magic circle recovered. 100 HP. 300 HP. 999 HP.

Each piece of the pattern slid into the slot where it was supposed to be, repairing itself! The magic circle was restored!

"All done. My ticket is secured."

"When did you learn all those kinds of healing magic...? I guess you've been leveling up, too."

"It's such a shame you can't see my true power on a daily basis."

"Well, if we don't need healing magic, that means we're adventuring safely. That should be a good thing, but I suppose that might pose something of an existential crisis for the party healer. So, uh…what's next?"

"Next is this! Here! Only one of these is the right one, so guess which!"

The cat beastkin angrily brought out ten magic circles.

"Well…if we appraise them, it should be easy."

"Yes! That's right! But it won't be easy! These magic circles are so hard to appraise, even the best antique dealer in Materville, the great Conno Sir (age seventy-four) failed to—"

"Yo, Porta."

"Yes! Leave it to me!"

Porta activated her Appraise skill. "Hmm…" She took a good long look at the identical magic circles, starting from the right.

"Got it! This one!"

She didn't even look at all of them. She just picked the fourth circle from the right.

The moment her hand touched it, the circle burst and turned into a ticket! She was right!

"I'm so happy! I got a ticket, too!" Yay!

"Porta's ranking her skills up like crazy, too. Tell this Conno Sir (age seventy-four) sorry, but Porta's perception is the best in the world! Mm, mm! I'm so proud!" Yay!

He lifted Porta up and spun her around. She smiled. Masato smiled. Everyone clapped.

And all events were cleared! Well done. Uh, wait.

"…Now, then."

Enough playing around. Masato put Porta down, straightened up, and fixed the cat with a glare.

Looking like a final boss reduced to his true form, the cat boy gulped.

"Fresh out of hospitality, huh?"

"Yeah…I'm way past welcoming any of you. Running this event smoothly is everything to me."

"Everything?"

"Everything. When this ends, I'll go back to being just another face in the crowd of NPC villagers. I can only fill a special role, be a special something, while this event is in progress."

"That does sound like a big deal..."

"And for you to just barrel through it like this... I'm gonna end it all. Override my welcome settings, summon the fiercest warrior the beastkin tribe has, and send you packing!"

"Th-the fiercest beastkin?! Seriously?!"

Final battle! The cat boy thrust an arm into the sky and yowled! "Meoooww!" "That meow is kinda ruining the tense mood!" Well, he *was* a cat. Don't worry about it!

A magic circle appeared on the ground. It was nothing like the previous circles—this one was clearly very intimidating. A roar shook the earth, and the summoned creature slowly rose out of it.

"The fiercest beastkin... No, whoever they are, I can beat them! I've been leveling up just like the others! Theoretically!"

Masato braced himself.

Triangular ears. A fluffy tail. Definitely a beastkin.

There were also five children clinging to her.

A fierce-looking glare...which widened into a grin the moment she saw them.

"Oh, Masato! My, my, Mamako, Wise, Medhi, and Porta, too! It's been ages!"

"Er...Growlette?"

Yep. It was Growlette, the beastkin mother who'd faced Mamako in the World Matriarchal Arts Tournament.

"Why is Growlette here...? O-oh, I suppose this *is* the beastkin world..."

"That's right! This is my world, and this is where I live...but I suppose this is no time for chitchat!"

She undid the strings that secured her children to her body.

"Okay, kids, Mom's got some work to do. You go play with the girls."

"Okay!" "Yay!" "Pway wif us!" "Pway!" "Girls!"

"Hey! Growlette! You can't... Oh, fine!"

"All right, over here with us. Behave!"

"I'll help! I'll help play!"

Wagging their tails, the beastkin kids rushed over to the girls.

Masato's party members were all too familiar with babysitting duty by now. "Panties!" "Don't flip girls' skirts!" "I'm going this way!" "Stay right here!" "I hafta pee." "Whaaat?!" But in no time at all, they were being run ragged anyway.

"…Now, then." Growlette straightened up, doing a few stretches, and turned to Masato. "Should we get started?"

"*Started*? …You mean we have to fight?"

"Yep! I took a job where I have to fight anyone I'm summoned in front of. It pays pretty well! So, yeah."

"…You can't be serious."

Growlette bent her knees a little and bared her claws—she was ready to attack. Her expression and body language made it clear she meant business.

Masato unsheathed his sword…but he couldn't turn it on Growlette! She was every bit as powerful as Mamako! There was no way he could win. That was part of it.

But even worse…

How can I fight Growlette? She's a mother!

He didn't mean to discriminate, but this was really bothering him.

He couldn't immediately think of a specific reason why, but it just felt *wrong*.

Masato glanced over at Growlette's children, and they were all staring wide-eyed up at him.

No! I can't fight her! Wh-what now?! …Oh, I know!

Eye for an eye, mom for a mom. Only way.

Backed into a corner, Masato was about to ask his mom for help, when…

"Just kidding! Here, take a ticket."

Growlette was waving a ticket at him.

"…Huh?"

"Ah-ha-ha! Gotcha! This was just a practical joke, making you think you had to fight someone from the World Matriarchal Arts Tournament! I was just trying to scare you a little—there's no need to actually fight."

"Uh…but I…"

"Here! Thanks for being such a sucker! Yay! Surprise!"

The cat boy was looking especially pleased with himself, leaning in and grinning, so Masato grabbed his whiskers and gave them a good yank. "Smile!" "Owww!" No mercy this time. He was straight up trying to pull them out.

Wise and Medhi approached him quietly from either side and elbowed him in the ribs.

"You were trying to get Mamako to step in for you, weren't you?"

"Wha…whatever do you mean? Ah-ha-ha…"

"I think that was the right decision. Leaving things to Mamako resolves every situation safely. I know just how you feel, Masato."

"Yeah, well…I just…"

He *had* been considering it.

But having this pointed out still stung.

When did it become so normal for me to rely on Mom?

And the fact that doing so had a proven track record of efficiency was all the more galling.

"Well, now we all have tickets! I suppose we should use them right away, don't you think, Ma-kun?"

"Er…uh…yeah, let's do that."

The cause of his current frustration remained oblivious to that fact, but he was no longer the kid who used to take that stuff out on her. He'd definitely grown up a lot!

He just let out a sigh and refocused. Time to use these tickets.

There was a DRAW button on the front of the ticket, and when he tapped it, a roulette effect appeared. The crowd of beastkin began beating their drums. Perhaps they were going for a sort of drum roll? Wrong kind of drums, though.

Then the ticket began glowing and changed shape! Draw complete! An item fell into Masato's hand.

It was a chain necklace that was threaded through a ring.

"This is… Uh, Porta? Can you appraise?"

"Okay! Hngg…this is…Guerriero's Necklace! When equipped, your attack goes up quite a lot! It's a warrior-class accessory, so you can equip it, Masato!"

"Oh…sounds like I hit the jackpot. Right, Whiskers?"

"I object to that nickname, but right you are! That item is at the top of the rarity pool."

"Oh my! Good for you, Ma-kun!"

"Seriously?! Hell yeah! My time has cooome!" Masato roared, getting a bit carried away.

"Wait, what? Masato got something? That doesn't make sense!"

"I was certain he was doomed to always fail at these things… How could you betray me like this?"

"Sheesh, some friends you two are…"

"If Masato can score, so can I! Here goes nothing!"

"Wise still doesn't stand a chance, but I will definitely score. Drawing…"

The two rude girls used their tickets, ignoring the beastkin children hanging off them. The roulettes spun.

Wise received a set of earrings engraved with magic sigils.

Medhi received a bracelet with a purple jewel.

"Oh! Earrings? The design's not too bad, either. I'm into it."

"My bracelet clearly has some unique effect. Porta, can you appraise it?"

"Sure! Hnggg…Medhi's bracelet is Night's Blessing! A Healer accessory, it allows you to absorb certain Dark attacks!"

"Wh-what?!" exclaimed Masato.

"Wait, that could be bad!" shouted Wise

Medhi already harbored plenty of dark power, so this could be a major power-up. "Might be too risky…" "Let's sell it while she isn't looking." "Over my dead body!" Medhi already had it equipped.

"It seems I've hit the jackpot. Wise, so sorry."

"For what? I probably hit the jackpot, too! …Porta, Porta, Porta! Appraise mine! Well? How are they?"

"Hngg…these earrings…wow! Congratulations, Wise! These are Prévenir! A Mage accessory that offers resistance against sealed magic!"

"………………Huh?!"

Wise froze, gawking at her earrings. Total mental shutdown. "Miss?" "You good?" The kids were playing under her skirt, but even that didn't get a reaction. She'd completely locked up.

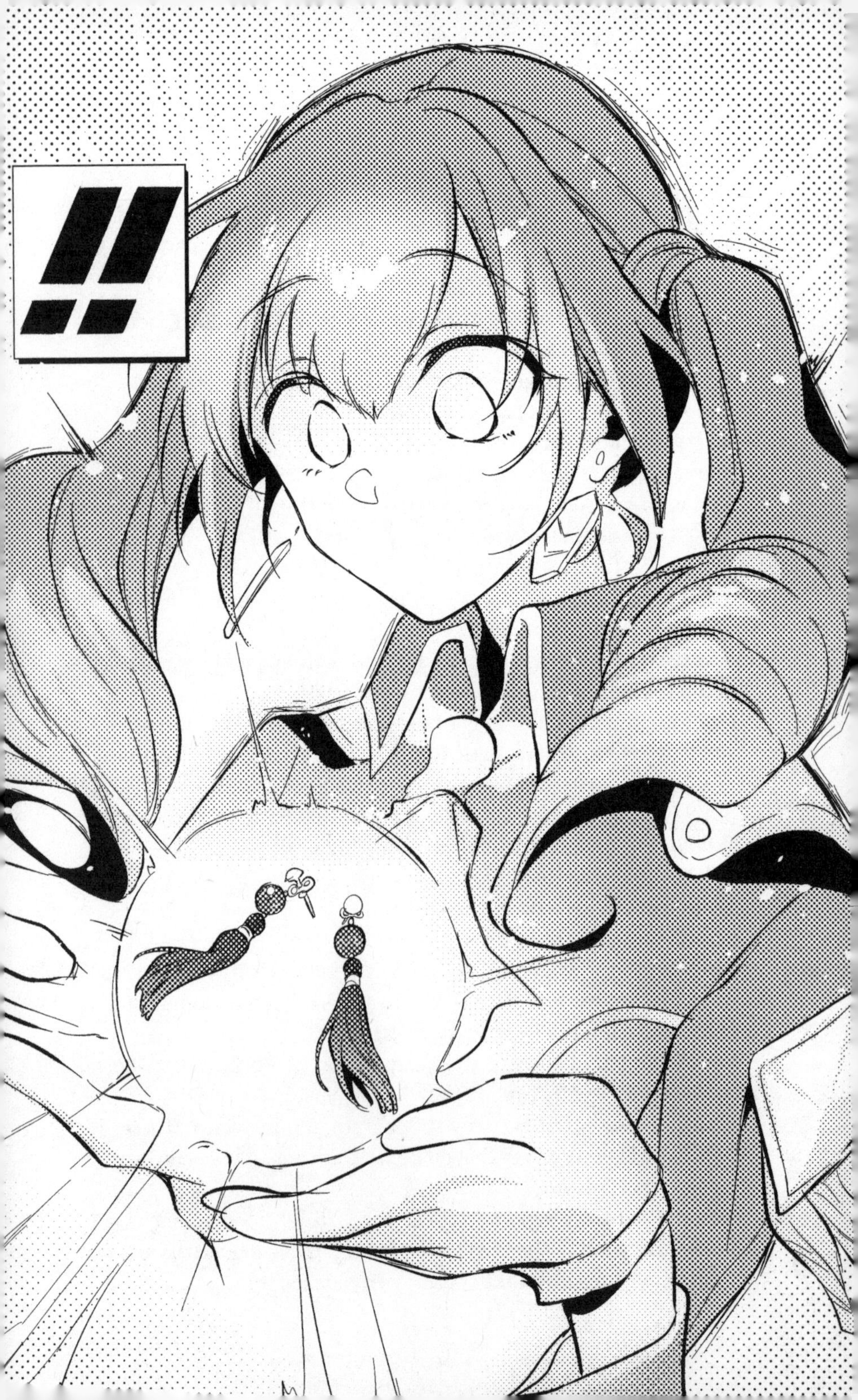
!!

"The one thing Wise needed most in all the world…and her mind can't even handle that much luck. Best to leave her alone for now…"

"Indeed. It's quieter like this. Let's hope she stays this way forever."

"But this means me, Medhi, and Wise got three hits in a row…"

"Only Mommy and Porta left! I wonder what we'll get!"

"I want something good! I'll try next!"

Porta put both hands together, made a wish, and then used her ticket.

The beastkin pounded their drums, and out popped…

"Wow, a ribbon! Hngg…this is…a Ribbon of Fortune! I can equip it! And it gives us 1.5× gem drops!"

"Wow! That's amazing! We'll be rich! Porta scored big, so that's four in a row! Go for a fifth, Mom! This event should end with total victory… I think…"

Weren't they getting a little *too* lucky?

It was worth bringing up. "Er, emergency meeting. Everyone but Mom." Medhi and Porta responded, and so did Growlette and the cat guy. Wise was still frozen, so they left her alone.

"I'm thinking there's something fishy going on here."

"Now that you mention it…every time we get in a situation like this, all of us fail, and only Mamako comes out ahead."

"So could this be the opposite?"

"Oh no! Only Mama's left out?"

"Don't be ridiculous! Nothing like that'll ever happen to Mamako," insisted Growlette. "Don't worry!"

"But the odds are getting pretty steep, right? You've all pulled four jackpots, and there's only one left. So…"

"If Mom wins, too, it'll be a real miracle…"

Would that miracle happen?

Only one way to find out.

"Okay… Mom."

"Got it! I'll draw… *Hyah!*"

Everyone gulped, watching. Mamako's roulette began spinning.

The ticket floated upward, glowing…and done!

A ticket-sized scrap of paper fluttered down onto Mamako's palm.

"A piece of paper… It doesn't say 'Try again,' does it?"

"Wait, Ma-kun! Look at this!"

"Huh?"

Mamako excitedly showed everyone the ticket. It read:

A three-night stay at a southern resort via airship!

Mamako had received a free vacation. All expenses paid, along with complimentary new outfits and a souvenir set.

"Three nights at a resort... That's..."

"Y-you got it!" the cat boy cried. "You actually got it! The event's grand prize! The biggest thing we have! The real jackpot! Congratulations!"

"Oh my! The grand prize? I'm so glad! Hee-hee."

A roar went up from the crowd. "Up you go!" "Oh my!" Growlette hoisted Mamako up on her shoulder. The drums and instruments all blared, and everyone was shouting.

At this flurry of cheers, Wise snapped out of it. "Huh? Oh, uh, thanks!" she said, assuming everyone was cheering for her. Let's just let the girl dream.

Everyone else was grinding their teeth.

"Mamako's the same as ever."

"Yep! She's still Mama!"

"I knew it. Everyone strikes out sometimes...except Mom. We never had a chance of beating her for the grand prize..."

At this point it just felt right. Part of him still resented it, but...at the very least, he could sigh and shrug it off.

Let the vacation commence!

No time like the present.

Masato was already changed into a Hawaiian shirt and shorts, ready to go.

"Okay, Whiskers! Which way? Hurry up!"

"Seriously, stop calling me that... But you're really excited about this, huh?"

"Well, yeah...wouldn't you be?"

The cat guy had led them to the southern end of Materville, the landing area for airships. Several flying ships were docked in this flat region along the coast, all bearing striking resemblances to simple-looking fishing boats, ornate cruise liners, and so on. The part people rode in was definitely boat-shaped.

These ship-like vessels had wings and propellers attached and were suspended from flying devices resembling balloons. They seemed less jet-propelled and more like they'd float away.

And...

"This is our airship?"

"Yes! You have the whole ship to yourselves. This is the grand prize package, so we spared no expense."

"Nice! You've got taste, at least."

The airship Masato's party would take was a beautiful, luxurious cruiser, sharply streamlined.

As a private vessel, it was smaller than the one they'd ridden as part of the school trip, but clearly much more expensive.

Even the letters *MTB* on the side were quite fancy looking.

"What does *MTB* stand for, anyway?"

"Mom Travel Bureau. The tour company that operates this airship... Oh, right. If you have travel vouchers from that company, you can use them to add options to the package at the local agency. Do you have any?"

"Probably? They sent some on Mother's Day, so Mom's probably got them... But that aside, we're flying this ourselves?"

"Yes. Like I said, it's all yours! There will be maps provided, and you'll find your own way to your destination. It's quite easy to fly, rest assured. I'll teach you how."

They went onto the ship deck to find a steering wheel in the center.

"Let me explain. Listen carefully. If you turn this wheel right, the ship will go right, if you turn it left, the ship will turn left, if you pull it up, the ship will rise, if you push it down, the ship will descend, if you push it forward, you'll speed up, and if you pull it back, you'll slow down. Simple, right?"

"You said all that almost spitefully fast, but I think I got it..."

Just then...

"Okay, we're ready! Where's the resort?!"

"Wise, no running ahead!"

"I'm so excited!"

The girls burst out of the ship cabins all dressed for a vacation.

"A southern resort... Finally, some downtime!"

Wise was wearing a loose tank top, seemingly no longer at all concerned about what this revealed about her bust (or lack thereof). Her hot pants were sliding down a bit, but the panties under them were clearly meant to peek out, so that was fine, too.

"Nothing says *southern* like the beach. And at the beach, you need to be careful about getting sunburned."

In contrast, Medhi was in full "rich girl at the beach" mode, showing less skin, but with fabric that was almost translucent, which really caught the eye. She carried a parasol, seemingly prepared to deal with both the sun and any onlookers.

"I've got beach toys and sunscreen!"

Porta was dressed to play in the water. In addition to her shoulder bag, she had an inner tube, a beach ball, and a whole lot more. With Porta around, they'd never want for things to play with.

"Sheesh, you're all getting ahead of yourselves."

"You changed before any of us, Masato! These things are all about enthusiasm."

"The fun of a vacation begins before you even leave. It's important to let loose immediately!"

"So, Masato! Should we go?"

"Well, if you're that impatient, Porta, let's... But there's still someone missing. Where'd she go?"

There was no sign of Mamako.

Then a couple of voices came from outside the airship. "You see, my kids..." "Ma-kun's the same way! That's why..." She was happily chatting with Growlette.

"Honestly, mothers! Geez. Hey, Mom! We're taking off in ten seconds! If you don't want us leaving you behind, get on board!"

"Oh my! Oh dear! I'll be right there!"

Mamako quickly turned and said, "I suppose it's about that time, Growlette." "Yeah, go on! Don't worry about souvenirs." "Oh no! If you want anything, just ask…" And they were already chatting again. Mothers were always like this.

By the time she finally stepped on board, Masato's eyebrow had developed a twitch.

"Ma-kun, everyone, I'm so sorry! It has been ages, and we just had so much catching up to do!"

She came running up the trap, breathing heavily.

Very little fabric covered her ample bosom, which was heaving prodigiously. She was in a swimsuit! So much skin! So much youthful sheen!

Masato had been about to give her a long lecture on the responsibilities of group travel, but this horror show banished *that*, and he settled for a long sigh.

"Mom…why are you in a swimsuit already?"

"I suppose I'm a little ahead of the party…sorry! But when I heard I could take a vacation with you, I just got so excited! I don't think we've done that together since you were in elementary school and the neighborhood children's club took that trip together! This is going to be great! Hee-hee!"

"Yeah, yeah, forget about that. Just go change…"

"Ack…I can't let Mamako win!"

"Let's go change into our swimsuits, too!"

"Yes! I want to change!"

"No, the three of you don't have to change! Calm down! I know you're excited, but take a breath!"

"Time to fly, bro! Aaand liftoff!"

"Yo, Whiskers, get out of here!"

"Dang, it didn't work… Well, bon voyage everyone!"

The cat boy grabbed the luggage he'd secretly snuck on board and slumped off down the trap.

Below, Growlette and her kids were waving their hands and tails, wishing the party a safe voyage.

"…Okay, off we go!"

Masato grabbed the wheel, and the ship's wings began to flap, the propellers spinning. He pulled it upward, and the ship began floating, slowly leaving the ground behind.

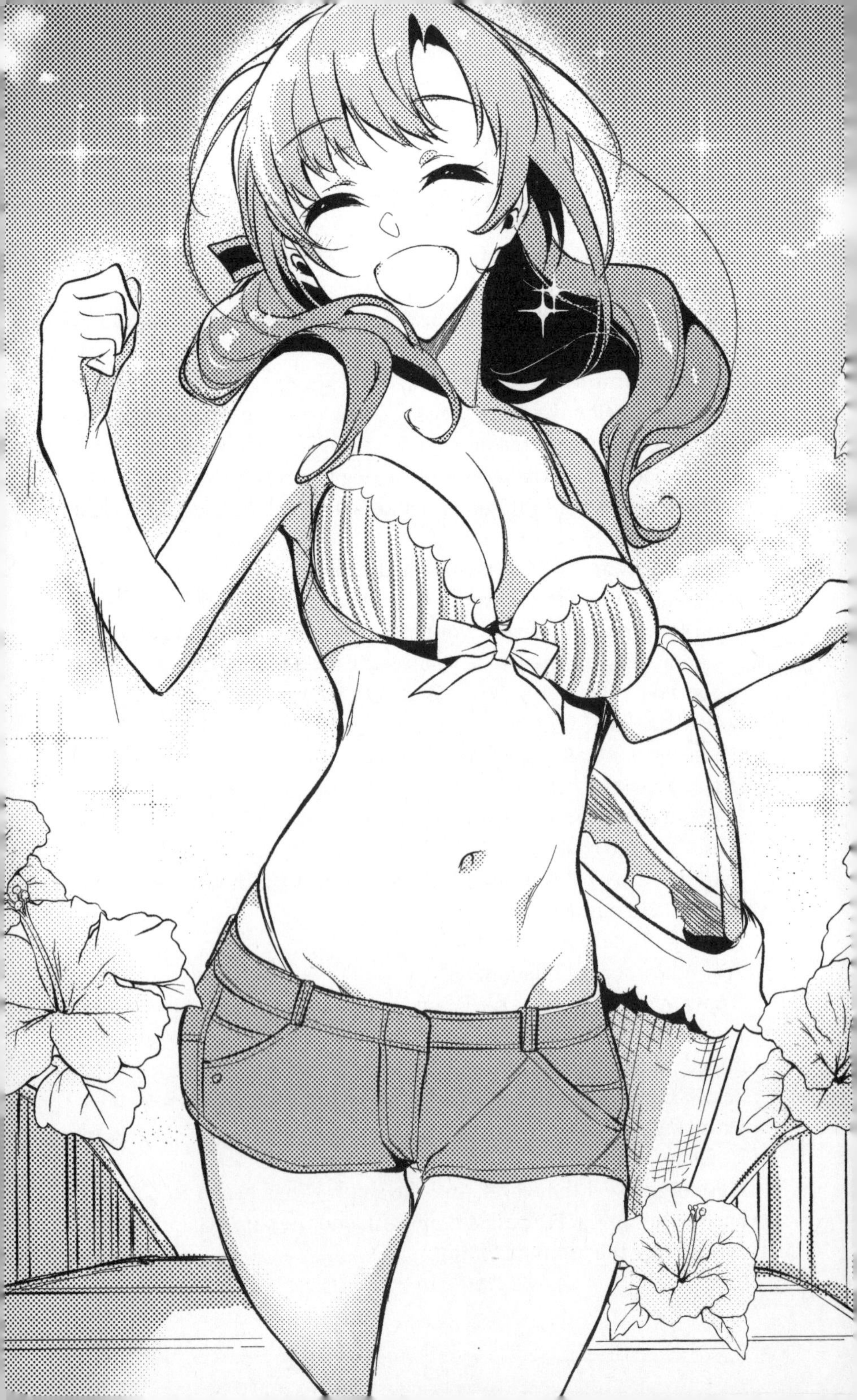

His first time flying an airship! He was a little nervous. He could feel his palms sweating.

But it was the most fun he'd ever had.

"This is great… I'm the hero of the heavens! I can do this! This is something I was meant to do! Leave the flying to me! You can all call me Captain! What do you say?"

"What're you gonna wear, Mamako?"

"Well, something breezy, I think."

"Perhaps something over the shoulders to keep the sun off you?"

"A short skirt is very breezy!"

"Ah-ha-ha, nobody's listening, but that's fine! I'm flying! Here we go!"

Women and fashion. Men and fantasy. To each their own, as they say.

With that, the airship ascended into the wild blue yonder.

The beastkin children trotted after the ship on their tiny legs, but there was no way they could keep up. Too bad.

The ship grew smaller before vanishing from sight.

"Well, they've taken off safely! Good, good. You did good work!"

"Glad to be of service." The cat boy hung his head. "Now I guess it's back to being part of the crowd! If you see me around town, be sure to say hi."

"Will do. But cheer up! You might get another shot!"

The cat boy wiped his tears away and walked off.

Growlette took her leave as well. Gathering up her wild children, she put a sling round them all and headed home.

Just then…

"Excuse me! You there, do you have a moment?"

"Mm? Who's asking?"

A human was running toward her. A woman with long hair, dressed in a nun's habit.

Growlette had seen her before.

"You were the emcee at the World Matriarchal Arts Tournament! You're an admin, right? Your name was…"

"Shiraaase. You've been a great help, and it's a pleasure to meet you again, Growlette."

"Gosh, how polite! So what brings you here?"

"I've been looking for Mamako. They said she'd come this way..."

"Oh dear. You just missed her! They just took off in an airship."

"I see... That's unfortunate..."

It was difficult to tell just *how* unfortunate this was, since Shiraaase was never one for facial expressions.

But Growlette's animal instincts were picking up on something.

"...Is there a problem?" she asked.

"Yes, well...there's going to be."

"'Going to be?'"

Growlette cocked her head. All five of her kids did, too.

This got a tiny smile out of Shiraaase, but it soon faded. She turned, staring into the distance.

"If I e-mail her, there's a risk they'll find out... I've got to meet with her in person, talk face-to-face. I'll have to use my admin skills to get there first...and get them mixed up in things. Heh-heh-heh."

"Hey, Mommy!" "She's a bad lady!" "Bad!" "No good!" "Evil!"

"You're right," said Growlette. "For Mamako and her party's sake, we'll have to eliminate this lady now."

"Let me rephrase. I shall politely request her assistance in this matter."

When Growlette still looked dubious, Shiraaase quietly fled, still staring.

On the deck of the airship flying gracefully through the cloudless sky...

"Erk... Did anyone else just feel a chill?" Masato shivered.

"Oh dear! It would never do to get sick on vacation. You should put my cardigan over your shoulders. Here!"

"Uh, no, don't need it! I'm fine! Hey!"

Masato's shoulders were already covered with the Mom cardigan. A horrible situation for any adolescent boy...!

It was soft and warm and smelled nice.

"Don't... Uh... That's way warmer than I thought..."

"That's the warmth of Mommy's love! Hee-hee!"

The reason Masato was so warm was because Mamako (now wearing a lightweight dress) was pressed up against his back, clinging to him. Lots of soft and warm going on there.

"Hey, Mom! Please don't do that!"

"But we can't have you catching a cold, Ma-kun."

"I appreciate the concern, but seriously, I'm fine! Even without that, I'm plenty warm."

Mamako was activating the special mom skill A Mother's Warmth.

The desire to keep your child from getting sick had created a barrier of warmth over the entire airship, completely shutting out the chilly wind that blew this high up.

Which was super helpful.

But stuff like this happens all the time, and I just take it for granted now...and Mom just gets even further ahead of me.

Masato was painfully aware of it, mad at himself for it, and quietly depressed by it.

He knew he couldn't keep going like this. He had to find his moment. He just needed something to happen that would give him a chance to shine. He was hoping for it, but then...

"Hey, helmsman-who-calls-himself-captain! Masato! Got a moment?"

"I'm going with 'small crew, everyone pulls multiple roles' as a justification, but what is it?"

After ribbing him a bit, Wise came over, holding the parchment with the map on it.

"Take a look here. We're heading due south from Materville, right?"

"Yep. I'm keeping us on course, don't worry. These hands hold steady and true, not letting the wheel drift right or left. Which is why I'm unable to brush away Mom or her cardigan."

"Captain Ma-kun works so hard! What a good boy." *Pat, pat.*

"And now she's petting me. But do you have any concerns about our course?"

"Sort of... It's nothing major, but..."

"Masato! I see an island!"

"We will soon be directly overhead."

"An island?"

Porta and Medhi had been looking over the stern, but they came running back to the wheel, and everyone looked at the map.

The map showed everything between Materville and the southern resort island. The terrain depicted was quite detailed, but...

"...There are no islands?"

"Exactly," said Wise. "There are some way out here, but not on our route."

"Yet, there actually is an island—a decent-sized one, too."

"Yes! I saw it with my own eyes! I didn't see any buildings or people, so it might be uninhabited!"

"We gotta trust Porta's eyes... Hmm, a deserted island..."

"Maybe they forgot to put it on the map?" offered Mamako.

"With something this big, I doubt they could have... I'm wondering if maybe there's some reason it isn't on there."

Like it was a secret island where pirates hid their treasure.

Or, given this game's genre, an island where a secret dungeon was hidden.

That could be cool.

Yo...yo yo yo yo yo, that sounds like the kind of adventure I've been hoping for!

Maybe this was Masato's awakening event?! Did this island hold his chance to free himself from his dependence on Mamako and stand on his own two feet? It sure spoke to the adventurer inside...

"Uh, Captain Masato..."

"You know what we're about to say."

"Erk..."

Wise and Medhi were both staring at him. He could already see the storm clouds forming over his parade.

But Mamako always had Masato's back, so he still had a shot! "Using Mamako..." "...is cheating." "Owwww!" Each of them pulled one of his ears, foiling this plan. He had never had a shot to begin with.

He had to choke back his tears and make the choice.

"…Fine. Then we'll stay on course for the resort. No landing on that island."

"For real? You'd better mean that, y'know. Look me in the eyes and promise."

This Sage didn't know what trusting friends meant. She peered into his face.

That was pretty annoying, so to pay her back, he flicked the earring she was wearing with one finger.

"Hey, what the hell?! You can't do that to my precious Prévenir! Don't you realize how much joy these have brought me?!"

"Yeah, yeah, sorry. Fair point."

He glanced sideways and saw that Medhi had the Night's Blessing bracelet on one arm. Porta had the Ribbon of Fortune on her head, too.

And Masato himself was no different; he'd equipped Guerriero's Necklace, the warrior gear he'd been dreaming of.

The fun vacation Mamako had won was now in full swing.

It was obvious what their priority should be.

"Right now, we've having the time of our lives, riding a wave of amazing luck. We've got to keep this going as long as we can! So let's just forget everything else and enjoy this vacation!"

A good leader always put the needs of his party first.

"Yeah, yeah, but what do you really want?"

"Be honest."

He'd only impressed Mamako and Porta. Wise and Medhi were just leaning in even closer, their eyes filled with suspicion.

"Hey! I definitely mostly meant that!"

"But you also thought an adventure on that island could be fun, right?"

"You were also hoping this would give you a chance to do more than Mamako for once, weren't you?"

"Gah…you sure know me well…"

"I knew it! Letting Masato fly us is too risky."

"He may well just decide to land us here! Mamako, you take over."

"No, wait! I'm flying this airship! I won't let anyone else handle flying stuff!"

Masato threw his arms around the wheel, clinging to it for dear life.

But Wise and Medhi would not allow it. "No tantrums!" "Be a good boy and let go!" "Nooo!" Each grabbed an arm, pulling hard...

And then came a snap.

""""...Uh?""""

"Oh my! That's not good!"

"Whoa! The ship's wheel came off!"

The wheel's axle had come off in Masato's arms. Masato, Wise, and Medhi turned pale, looking at one another. A moment later...

A sideways gust of wind hit the ship, and it lurched to the right. There was no way for them to straighten it out.

"Uh...aughhhh! We're falliiiiing!"

They slid across the deck...and were flung out into open air.

They were in free fall. Their descent became faster and faster, and the ground grew rapidly closer.

But they'd been pretty high up. They still had quite a while before that unpleasant impact.

"Aughhhh! The wind force is crazyyyyyy! My face huuurts!"

"Ma-kun! Turn your back to the ground! It won't hurt so much that way!"

"Oh, you're right. But that doesn't solve the main problem! ...Oh yeah! Wise! You used a floatation spell that time we fell in a cave, right?! Can you slow our descent?"

"I don't have my tome equipped! I can't use any magic! Medhi?!"

"I gave my staff to Porta! I can't cast any spells, either!"

"I wish I could give them to you, but if I take anything out of my bag, it'll get blown awaaaaay!"

"Then, Mom... Wait, no!"

They were in midair.

"This is the moment! The hero chosen by the heavens will reveal his power! Right! Grant me the power to give everyone wings! Hahhh!"

He struck a hawklike pose, concentrating his mind! His companions would sprout wings!

They did not.

"I knew iiiiiiiiiiiiiiit! We're falliiiiiiiiiiiiiiiiing!"

The party fell straight down…to the uncharted island.

Approximately half the island was mountainous. The other half was covered in green, with a broad, sandy beach.

The airship had been flying over the green bit. That coincidence was the closest thing to luck they had.

"We're doooooooomed! We're gonna diiiiiie!" shrieked Wise.

Also lucky: The forest was made of giant broccoli.

The clusters of green flower heads gently caught everything that fell onto them.

"Aiiiieee… Oh… Are we safe?" asked Medhi. "Ack, I spoke too soon!"

They'd avoided being flattened, but they weren't done falling yet.

They went rolling across the rounded tops and then fell to the broccoli below. Bouncing off one round flower head after another, spinning wildly…

"Whoa! My bag caught on something! …Augh! And my clothes! And my underwear! …Eeeek!"

By the time the ground was finally in sight, everyone had been stripped.

Wise, Medhi, and Porta landed face-first. End of the line.

"Mmph! Wh-what the heck is this?!" cried Wise.

"It's like a giant, soft mushroom," said Medhi.

"Not that, I mean…!"

"Is everyone okay? Anyone hurt?" *Boing, boing!*

Mamako's boob cushions—the girls had been caught by these incredibly bouncy orbs and had all landed safely.

There were relieved hugs all around, and that's when they realized…

"I can feel Mamako's warmth seeping into me… Wait, why are we naked?!"

"It seems we lost all our equipment in the fall…"

"I—I don't have my bag, either! I think it got caught on something up there! W-w-we have to find it!" Porta looked ready to run off blindly.

"Don't worry, Porta," Mamako said, giving her a big hug and patting her on the back. "First, let's all calm down. Okay?"

Porta wiped away her tears and calmed down a little.

"Wait! My Prévenir?! They're goooone! Aughhh! No, no, no! Noooo-ooooooooooooooooooooooooooooooooooooooooooooooooooooooooo!"

"Don't worry, Wise. First, take a deep breath... Hahhh!"

"Gah!"

When Wise had started to freak out, Medhi had smacked her on the back of her head. "Mm? What was I yelling about?" "Something best forgotten." Wise was calmed down forcibly.

Now everyone was calm.

"Wise, Medhi, Porta! You're all safe, thank goodness... That just leaves...M-M-M...Where's Ma-kun?! Ma-kun! Ma-kuuuuun?!" Panic time!

"Oh yeah, I don't see Masato...uh, Mamako? Calm down!!"

"I'm sure Masato's fine, so let's do something about the nudity first."

"We can make clothes out of leaves! ...Whoa! Mama, waaait!"

Mamako rocketed away like a bullet. There were massive broccoli stalks and bountiful vegetation everywhere, but she didn't care. She just raced straight through them, still naked.

"Ma-kun! Ma-kun, where are you?! Ma-kuuun! Maaaaaaaaaaaa-kuuuuuun!!"

The voice of a mother crying for her son echoed through the jungle.

"Hmm... Did I hear...? Ack!"

Feeling like he'd heard Mamako calling, Masato opened his eyes.

He was lying on the ground, miraculously unharmed, despite having fallen off an airship.

He'd been knocked out, and his head was still spinning a bit. But he was otherwise intact. Nothing was hurting anyway. He could feel grass under his back. Directly. "Crap, I'm naked!" Had his clothes caught on something?

"You okay there, sonny?"

*   *   *

"…Huh?"

Masato heard a cute, gentle voice. He looked up and saw someone standing over him.

They were a little bigger than Porta—definitely on the small side—and wearing tribal leather clothing and a grass skirt. Their short hair was a dull shade of white.

The face below that was…definitely cute. A slight blush on it.

Seeing this new person avert their eyes, Masato remembered his condition, grabbed a leaf, covered himself, and sat up.

"Um…are you a native…girl?"

"I will butcher you!" The person snarled and narrowed their eyes. Their face and voice were still cute, but…the anger was genuine.

"S-sorry…you're a boy, then?"

"You betcha. My name's Fratello. I'm an extremely manly man, the kind who moseys off to a deserted island for secret survival training. And who might you be, sonny…?"

"Uh, right, my name's Masato…"

"Mm? Wait."

Masato had been about to explain his predicament, but the ground underfoot started shaking.

Whoom. Whoom. Wh-whoom. The shaking was intensifying. The source of it was getting closer…and a moment later, something leaped over the brush nearby, shaking everything around and looming over Masato and Fratello.

It was a frog the size of a single-story house, with some dangerous-looking horns.

"A horned frog! That's a big 'un."

"A monster?! But it's too big! And I'm naked, ugh!"

"Perhaps you oughtta take my grass skirt. Go on, equip it. I still have leather pants, don't worry."

Fratello removed the grass skirt and handed it to Masato. "Thanks!" It was a little small, but wearable. And still kinda warm…

Masato's defense went up by 1!

"Wow, that's some crappy armor…b-but better than nothing! Now I just need to equip a stick, and…right, let's do this!"

"You lookin' to fight this thing, sonny?"

"W-well, honestly, I don't have much hope, but...what choice do we have? I'm not running away! I'm a man!"

"Well said. But I won't be needin' your help. A single blow from me'll wrap this up right quick. Mahhhhhhh!" Fratello summoned his menacing aura!

"Whoa, what the heck was that shout?! It's so cute! But that aura is no joke..."

Fratello stood before the horned frog, striking a pose like a karate master, charging his power. His little hands clenched tight, focusing his energies.

Fratello attacked!

"Mahhhhhh...mm!"

Fratello released a deadly strike!

His fist dented the frog's belly...

...and with a sound like an explosion—like something breaking the sound barrier—the frog went flying. It tore through the jungle and was already gone from sight.

The hole it left behind stretched into the distance, the plants still shaking in the frog's wake.

"...Huh?"

"Mm, not half bad."

The power demonstrated was not exactly something you'd call *not half bad* with a straight face.

Fratello flexed his little hand a bit, as if testing it, then turned to Masato.

"Ya got guts fer doin' this survival trainin' without a stitch on, but pick your battles. This island has heaps of monsters. Watch yourself, sonny!"

"Uh, yeah, got it."

"Mm. Bye."

Fratello left.

"Uh, Fratello!"

"Mm?"

"That was an amazing strike! Really badass! Hella manly!"

Masato meant every word.

Fratello turned bright red, like he was utterly delighted, snapped out a thumbs-up, and then vanished through the hole in the jungle. Definitely supercute for a boy.

Masato just watched his tiny back until he was gone…

Then.

"Uh, wait… Should I have let him go?"

After all, Masato had crashed on this island. He was stranded here. With no equipment.

Would he be in trouble without assistance from someone who already knew the island well? Yep, big trouble. He was totally screwed. Masato felt the blood draining from his face.

And then…

"I can sense Ma-kun this way! I'm sure he is! Over here!"

"You keep saying that, but we aren't finding him anywhere! Seriously, calm down!"

"You're so worked up, your Masato Sensor isn't working!"

"Mama! Please calm down a little! Pleeeease!"

"Those voices…!"

Rapid footsteps came from the brush nearby.

Around the approaching figures' waists were skirts made of leaves. Chest guards made of braided grasses and island flowers covered their torsos. They wore leaves woven into sandals on their feet. Altogether, they looked like beautiful jungle spirits… It was Wise, Medhi, Porta, and…

…running at top speed, Mamako.

"Ma-kun! There you are! Ma-kuuun!"

"Oh, glad to see you're all safe… Wait, stop! No need for hugging!"

This proved useless. "Ma-kun!" "Oof!" He was swept into an embrace.

It was a powerful, merciless squeeze from a mother who'd found her missing son at last, his face held so tight to her chest that he couldn't breathe.

"Guh! A-are you trying to kill me?!"

"What? Ma-kun, were you in mortal peril?! Oh no! Well, Mommy will hold you tighter until you come back to life!"

"That doesn't even make sense! That's the greatest threat to my life!"

"Mamako, seriously, calm down! We've found Masato already! Relax! Please, just chill out, okay?!"

Wise, Medhi, and Porta all desperately appealed to her, and Mamako finally started to settle down.

"S-sorry... Mommy just got so worried..."

"I appreciate the concern, but you first need to stay calm and assess the situation. Everyone's safe, right?"

They all nodded. That alone was a relief.

He didn't need to check twice; they'd all clearly lost their clothes. Those beach outfits had been rentals...but, well, they could deal with that later.

When Masato realized Porta was missing her bag, he almost said something, but quickly thought better of it. Porta would be the most upset by that. Once glance at her face showed she was.

So we've lost everything, and we're on a deserted island...

Well, except for...

"Uh, so, listen, I actually just met this boy. His name's Fratello. Kinda looks more like a girl, but he's definitely a guy."

"What, seriously?" said Wise. "People live here?"

"No, he said he was here for survival training. Otherwise this place is uninhabited."

"So he's insane," said Medhi. "That said, he probably knows a lot about the island and how to get by here, so that would certainly be helpful... Where is he?"

"W-well... Uh... He was here a moment ago, but I don't know where he went."

Wise's and Medhi's eyebrows snapped together. They gave Masato a long, reproachful glare.

Even Masato himself thought they were right this time.

"S-so my point is—"

"You'd better not say it's time for an adventure on a deserted island."

"Or that you want to do some survival training like this boy is doing."

"No, uh, it's not like we have a choice here! We don't know where

Fratello went, so we can't just look for him, and even if we try, the sun'll be down soon..."

"And this conveniently gives you an excuse to try the adventure you wanted."

"Was the entire 'falling off an airship' thing just Masato's clever scheme?"

"That was an accident! And that only happened because you two—no, never mind. Point is, if we're gonna survive this, there are steps we have to take!"

Secure food and water and shelter. These were their priorities.

And yeah, I'm a bit excited to try this survivalist thing!

Masato's life had been under Mamako's protective wing so long, and this adventure could be a chance to stretch his own wings.

If Fratello could do it, so could Masato. There was a little rivalry going on there, too.

But whatever Masato's motivations, he was right about what they needed.

"Yes...Mommy thinks Masato's right."

"Oh! See? Mom gets it! You go, Mom!"

"Hee-hee. Thank you. Let's begin!"

"Yeah! Here we go! Risking our lives to survive! Don't worry! This is where it helps to have a man around! I'll take care of... Wait, Mom? Where are you...?"

Mamako had suddenly run off and was feeling around in the brush.

Looking closely, he saw daikon, carrots, tomatoes, cucumbers—all very familiar vegetables. They were unfamiliar sizes and shapes, but... Oh, there were apples and tangerines, too.

"Now that I'm having an honest look around, it seems there's lots of edible food in this jungle! That's such a relief. Hee-hee."

Provisions: secured.

"Uh...well, food's no big deal! Not in a vegetable jungle! B-but I'm sure finding water will be a challenge! Let me handle—"

"I wonder if I can ask for water even now that I've lost that Holy Sword? ...Mother Earth...please," Mamako said, placing her palms on the ground. "Without water, awful things could happen to these precious children... Lend me your power..."

There was a long groove in the ground in front of them, and as they watched, it became covered in round stones, like a riverbed, and then water gushed up—in the blink of an eye, they had a freshwater stream.

"I hope this water's safe to drink! Porta, dear, can you appraise it?"

"Yes! Hngg…this is very clean water! We can definitely drink it!"

Water: secured.

"Seriously? You can use the power even without the swords? That's ridiculous… Rrgh… Okay, fine! Shelter! We've got to cut down some trees and put it all together! Lots of hard work involved! It's safe to say this was a trial meant for—!"

"Mother Earth, if I may make one more request… So that these children can sleep peacefully in this jungle, we'd like some sort of home… Please, lend us your strength."

Mamako was at it again.

The giant broccoli stalks nearby cut themselves down, turning into construction supplies.

"…Uh?"

Then the resulting lumber put itself together without any nails, like the handiwork of a master temple carpenter…and formed a lovely cottage, three stories tall, with broad verandas like a luxury villa.

Shelter: secured.

"…………Huh?"

"Wow! That house was built so quick!" marveled Porta.

"Okay, everyone! Let's go inside!"

"Mamako, you're so reliable! C'mon, Masato."

"Masato, time to go."

"………………Uh, yeah…"

Wise and Medhi smiled gently, patted him on the shoulders, and gave him a push toward the cottage interior.

The boards didn't even creak underfoot—that's how sturdily built this place was. There were several rooms inside.

The living room had a wooden table and a couch made of leaves. The house even came furnished!

"Oh, and clothes!" noted Wise. "Several sets! Awesome!"

"The same designs as the vacation clothes we were wearing!" said Medhi.

"Mother Earth is so thoughtful! Such a help. Let's get changed right away! I wonder if there's a bath. We could always change in one of the bedrooms, too."

"I'll go check the other rooms!" volunteered Porta.

"Hee-hee! Yes. Let's change, check the rooms, and then eat!"

The girls all grabbed clothes and left the living room, chatting as they went.

And…

Masato fell backward onto the couch, staring at the ceiling.

"………………………………………………………………So much for survivalism…"

A single tear rolled down his cheek.

At that exact time, outside…

Two figures were staring at the cottage.

"You're sure it was Mamako Oosuki's party inside?"

"They were wearing leaves and grass for cloooothes, but it was deeeefinitely them."

The faces peering through the brush were those of a girl with an expression as fierce as a tiger, and one with languid, downturned eyes.

They were on all fours, their heads hidden, their behinds not. Hard to imagine from this posture that these were two of the Libere Rebellion's Four Heavenly Kings, Amante and Sorella.

"I thought I saw someone falling off an airship passing overhead, but I never imagined it would be Mamako Oosuki…"

"And she built suuuuch a nice cottage. Whatever foooor? She's sooo annoying… What nooooow? Should we attaaack?"

"Yeah… None of them were armed, and I didn't see Porta's bag…so this might be our best shot, but…"

Amante thought about it, then shook her head.

"No, we can't do it. If we attack directly, they'll know we're here. We need to avoid that. After all, this island…"

"Yes, yeeees. You don't need to explaaaain. I already knoooow. That would definitely be baaad. We can't have aaaanyone searching the island wondering why we're here."

"We need Mamako Oosuki's party to leave the island without noticing us. How can we make that happen? Any ideas?"

"Hmm... Not off the top of my heeead..."

The two of them looked at each other.

"Then we should head back? Have the three of us talk it over?"

"That's riiiight. Three heads are better than twoooo. I think that's the expressiiiiion."

"I think it's 'Three's a crowd.'"

"Saaay, is it just meee, or does it feel a bit muddy here to youuu?"

They backed out of the brush and walked away—to meet up with the third Heavenly King.

The Hero Masato Oosuki's Ultimate Move Development 1

I think I need some sort of ultimate move if I'm ever gonna really show off what I've got... Do you have one, Wise? Other than getting your magic sealed.

That's hardly an ultimate move. Jerk. But I have chain casting, which is *way* better than anything you have, loser.

WISE

Chain casting... Two spells in a row... So a two-hit attack. That's actually pretty good for someone like you.

Ha! You want me to teach it to you? Then bow before me and say, "Pretty please, O Magnificent Wise!" C'mon!

WISE

Nah, no thanks. It'd suck if I ended up learning the art of getting my attacks sealed like you do.

It's not an art!

WISE

Chapter 2 Since We're Living Here Now, the Uninhabited Island Is Technically Inhabited, but Pay That No Mind.

Their first morning on the uninhabited island...

Masato woke up early, got out of his (very comfortable) bed, changed into a Hawaiian shirt and shorts, and quietly left his room.

"No trace remains of the whole 'survival on a deserted island' thing...but I can't let this situation get the best of me... I have to put myself in a harsh environment and make myself stronger without relying on my mom! Then I can accomplish at least *one* thing on my own..."

His mind made up, he started for the front door.

He was channeling his inner lone wolf...

"Oh, Ma-kun! You're up early! Are you heading out for your usual morning training?"

Mamako had poked her head out of the kitchen, where she was busy making breakfast.

"Uh, no, mostly looking for Porta's bag. Might do a little light training on the way."

"Don't go too far! Mommy's making a very tasty breakfast! Take care out there."

"Uh, yeah...I will."

He couldn't bring himself to say he didn't need breakfast. And feeling like a well-fed pet was not pleasant.

First, he had to find this bag. Masato made his way through the jungle around the cottage. Leaves wet with morning dew slipped past him.

"Ugh... it's colder than I expected... Ew, a spiderweb! Augh, what the hell is that bug?!"

Direct contact didn't spook him or anything, but it could be dangerous, so he picked up a stick and started pushing the vegetation aside.

He searched around the cottage, gradually widening his search range until he couldn't see the building anymore...but didn't find the bag.

"I knew it wouldn't be that easy. Ah, well. That's enough bag searching for the day...time for some training."

He found a decent clearing and held the stick up high.

Eyes forward, mind focused.

Feel it... The man within... The wild power...

Just as his spirits reached a fever pitch...

There was a rustle from the brush nearby. "Who's there?" Masato quickly raised the stick and swung it toward the sound.

A pair of tiny hands shot out of the brush, ready to catch the stick!

Donk. Only after it hit did the hands clap together.

"Heh... Good swing, sonny."

His stick had hit a head full of dull white hair—Fratello. There was a faint glimmer of tears in the boy's dazed-looking eyes.

"Yo, I thought you were a monster! ...Er, sorry about tha—"

"Gotcha!"

The moment he tried to apologize, Fratello shot out of the brush—"Mah!" "Wha?!"—and tried to punch him in the face.

Masato had been about to bow his head, but he quickly jerked it up, avoiding a direct hit.

"Whoa, whoa! I was trying to apologize! Nice manners you got there."

"This here's how men greet each other! Come at me, sonny!"

"Whoa, hang on... I owe you for saving me earlier..."

"Gratitude ain't gonna make me stronger. But joining me in my morning training? Now that's what I'm talkin' about. C'mon, sonny, do your worst. I won't hit ya too hard."

This offer annoyed Masato.

Fratello likely intended it to. He was grinning from ear to ear.

"Oh yeah?" Masato said. "Then let's go."

As out of it as this boy seemed sometimes, he sure knew how to drop a challenge. Masato gladly accepted it.

He adjusted his grip on the stick. Fratello rolled up the sleeves of his leather tribal garb; he was ready.

Both braced themselves. And then…

"Mah!"

Fratello's fist went for Masato's chin.

The blow was swift, but his reach just wasn't enough. Masato took a step back and dodged.

"This is how real men greet each other, right? I won't hold back!"

"That's the spirit, sonny!"

Masato took a quick step in and a sideways swing…but…

Fratello was even quicker than he looked. His tiny body left the ground, jumping higher than Masato's eyeline and sending a kick toward his face.

Masato's arms shot up, blocking and pushing back.

"Mahh?"

"Too bad! Flying enemies are *mine*!"

With Fratello off balance in midair, Masato attacked, his stick striking dead center on the boy's belly!

Fratello took 1× damage!

"Huh? My attack only did 1× damage?! Whaaat?!"

"That was downright wimpy. Now's my turn… Mahhhh!"

Fratello began charging, a powerful aura concentrating within his fist.

The same attack that had easily blown away a giant monster!

I can't soak that head-on! Gotta dodge!

Masato quickly backed away, but Fratello moved fast, closing the gap.

Fratello swung!

"Mahh!"

With a weird little yelp, his unleashed his ultimate attack! Direct hit to Masato's abdomen!

Masato took 1× damage!

"Uh…only 1× damage?"

"I thought so… My moves don't work right against ya… Grrr…"

"Are your attacks only effective against certain opponents? And totally tragic against anything else?"

"Mm." Fratello nodded.

He was honest, at least.

"And you called *me* wimpy? You're *way* wimpier."

"No I'm not! I can still rough up a whippersnapper like you without breakin' a sweat. Just not at the moment. Ain't got my equipment."

"W-well, I don't have my gear, either! Not right now anyway. That's why I can only do 1× damage! That's what's going on here!"

They were the same level. The same sad level.

This mutual admission had brought them closer, at least.

"Anyway, now we know... Ha!"

"Mah!"

Masato's stick slipped past Fratello's guard, smacking him in the side.

But Fratello stood his ground, punching Masato in the side as well. Payback.

Both combatants took 1× damage!

Yep. They were evenly matched and equally low level.

"Mah! Mah! Mah!"

"You little... Why I oughta... Hey!"

Masato sliced downward! Fratello nimbly evaded!

Fratello thrust his fist out! Masato blocked with the stick!

Masato went for a diagonal slash! It struck Fratello's shoulder! 1× damage!

Fratello scored a body blow! Masato was hit in the abdomen! 1× damage!

Fratello...you're the best! You're the rival I've been searching for!

Same here, sonny... Fighting a young fella my level is the most fun I've ever had.

As they continued to trade blows, they spoke with glances alone—two warriors, equally leveled, their ferocious battle spanning hours...

Or at least, that's how it felt. In truth, it had only been around ten minutes.

"*Hahh...hahh...* I...I think that's...enough for today..."

"I...I'll let ya off...with that... Be grateful, sonny... Mahhh..."

Both boys fell to the ground, utterly spent.

They basked in the afterglow of battle, both completely unharmed, riding the high of meeting their perfect rival.

Then Fratello stood up.

"…Going already?" asked Masato.

"Mm. I've confirmed the location in question. Met you, did some sparrin'. I've handled all the business I had this morning."

"*Location*? …No, never mind. Men don't sweat the small stuff."

"Mm. You're a real man, sonny. You get it." Looking quite pleased, Fratello turned to leave. "Oh, right," he said. "There are some real troublemakers roaming this island. Watch yourself, sonny."

"Troublemakers? I dunno who you mean, but okay. I'll watch out."

"Mm. Farewell, my equal match…k-kindred spirit."

Fratello snapped a thumbs-up and raced off. He expression appeared slightly dazed, and he seemed to be blushing a bit.

"Kindred spirit? The heck is he even saying? Geez…"

Masato shook his head, looking secretly pleased. He, too, raised a thumb.

"Hum hummm, hum hum hummm, kiiindred spiiiiriiit…"

"Ma-kun, you've been in such a good mood since you got back! Did something good happen?"

"Yeah, kinda. To put it mildly, I'm in the best mood. Ha-ha."

"Well, that's lovely! Hee-hee."

It was time for breakfast. Laid out on the dining room table (there were chairs, too) were rice, miso soup, fried river fish, and lightly pickled veggies. They were even served on real dishes, not plates made of leaves or anything.

"The cottage came complete with rice, miso, dashi, and dishes? Man, the power of Mother Earth sure is incredible. This doesn't even count as roughing it… But hey, that's fine! Ha-ha! Oh, is this sweetfish? The grated daikon and soy sauce sure go well with rice! Ha-ha-ha!"

"Make sure you get enough to eat! …Oh my, I'd better make our lunches!"

Masato was all smiles, thoroughly enjoying himself and plowing through breakfast. Next to him, Mamako plucked a grain of rice off her son's cheek and ate it adorably.

Meanwhile, across from them, the three girls were getting suspicious.

"What's going on? Yesterday he was all 'My survivalist life is doomed' and totally despondent."

"And now he's oddly cheery... Did he eat some weird mushroom that's made him delusional? Porta, can you detect anything?"

"Hmmm... No weird status effects! Masato's totally normal!"

"He clearly isn't! This is obviously abnormal!"

"Whew... That was a great meal! Thanks, Mom!"

"I'm so glad you liked it."

Totally ignoring their inquisitive looks, he washed down the morning the Japanese way—with green tea. *Slurrrrp.* "Hah..." Bliss.

So. With the meal done and the table cleared, Masato started the discussion.

"Everyone ready? We'd better talk about our plans. What? You want to hear my idea? Cool, happy to share."

"I didn't ask."

"I know, I know, just hear me out. We've lost our luggage. So our first order of business is to find Porta's bag."

"Yes! We have to find it!"

"But it won't be easy to locate. We don't have clear memories of where we landed or how we moved from that spot."

"Because Mommy panicked and ran all over! I'm so sorry."

"No, no, this is perfect... *Cough, cough...* I—I mean, since the search will be a difficult one, we'll be forced to stay on this island for the time being. Everyone agrees, right? Right?"

He beamed at all of them, awaiting their agreement.

Wise was getting even more suspicious. "Girl squad, assemble," she said. Everyone but Masato began whispering.

"Does Ma-kun want to stay here for a while?"

"Seems like it... I'm sure he's got his reasons, but—"

"Whatever that is, it's perfect for us. We should probably fill him in."

"Yes! I'm sure Masato will agree!"

"Mm? What? What's going on?"

The girls all lined up before him.

"Well, Ma-kun, we have something we want to ask you."

"Ask me? Um, okay. Lay it on me."

"Last night, while you were dead, we got to talking…," Medhi began.

"Why don't we turn this island into a resort and have our vacation here?" said Porta.

"Turn the island into a resort…? Vacation…?"

The girls all beamed at him.

"It's got water, food, and perfect weather!" said Wise.

"Everything we need to live, surrounded by untouched nature… This place is far better than some dumpy resort area," added Medhi. "So…"

"You want to open a new one? No, no, that would be a ton of work. How would we…?"

"Don't be dumb, Masato. Did you forget who we have with us?"

Wise, Medhi, and Porta all gathered around, fluttering their hands at *her*, like they were trying to demonstrate how much she sparkled. It almost worked.

Mamako—the *her* in question—smiled.

"The whole point of our journey was to have a vacation! But after that accident, we have no way of getting to the southern island… This place would make a great replacement!"

"And your mom powers will easily develop this resort…?"

"Oh, but we're not going to destroy the environment or anything. We'll make sure to ask Mother Earth not to force it at all. But if we open the jungle up some, it'll make it easier to find the bag."

"Mamako doesn't want to use her mom power too much," explained Medhi. "So we'll be hunting for the bag ourselves while we develop the land."

"We'll make our own resort, find my bag, and have a celebratory vacation! What do you think, Masato?"

Grins, excitement, sparkles. The girls all looked expectant.

Masato's brain went into overdrive.

Mom's gonna unleash her powers again… I'm not a fan of that, but…

If they were vacationing here, that meant he could stay longer.

And finding the bag themselves worked for him.

A competitive treasure hunt with him…*could be fun.*

He was sure Fratello would be all, "Perfect. That's the sort of thing that stirs a man's soul, sonny." The two of them would compete like real men and deepen their friendship.

Not bad at all. Actually, it sounded pretty great. Masato nodded. "Okay, then…"

"I mean, it's not like it matters what Masato thinks. The moment Mamako was on board it was a done deal. Let's get this resort started!"

"Hey, I didn't even finish! …Fine, whatever. I'm used to it by now… Oh, right! I ran into Fratello again this morning, and—"

"Let's go! We should start at the beach," said Medhi.

"Yes," agreed Mamako. "If we're looking for the bag, we should head into the forest…but there's something I'd like to check on at the beach first."

"If Mama's curious, I'm curious! I don't mind starting there!"

"Uh, hello? Is anyone listening? He said there are troublemakers on the island—"

"Let's build the best resort ever! First…we'll need a place to swim!"

""""Yeah!!""""

"Yeah! …No, seriously, people! Listen!"

They seemed ready to leave Masato behind.

The party left the cottage and headed to the water's edge, relying solely on their sense of direction. "So many leaves!" "Oh, a monster!" "Go away! Shoo!" "Am I gonna get to do anything?" "Oh my!" Jungles and monsters were no obstacle between a group of girls and a resort.

But they were a little too focused on the resort, and never noticed…

…the pairs of eyes watching them.

"…They're on the move."

"Indeed, they're quiiiite eager."

Amante and Sorella had been lurking in the brush by the cottage.

"They're going toward the beeeach… Whyyy?"

"I don't know…but we can't have them poking their noses everywhere."

"Riiight. The beach isn't a proooblem. But if they go into the woooods…or beyooooond…that would be baaad."

"We've gotta drive them off this island first…by posing as mysterious locals."

Amante pulled a strange mask made of leaves out of her bag and equipped it.

She was already dressed for the part—instead of her Libere Rebellion coat, she was wearing tribal clothing made from leather.

Sorella donned a similar mask, and their disguises were complete.

"I don't need to explain our plan to you, do I?"

"We pretend to be locals and say, 'This island is our sanctuary! Begone, outsiders!' and make them leeeave. I knoooow already."

"But if worse comes to worst, we'll have to force them. So be ready... Mm?"

There was a sound behind them. Something was coming through the grass.

The first thing they saw was...a spear? No, a horn.

A long, sharp, gleaming horn and a fat canary-yellow body.

A bug the size of an elephant—a Hercules beetle.

"A monster? Heh-heh-heh. Perfect. We'll ride this and catch Mamako Oosuki's party off guard."

"Ooooh... That does make us seem like locals with mysteeeerious powers. Niiiice. I'm iiiin!"

The two of them hopped onto the beetle's head.

And they were off!

"Okay, Sorella! Order this thing to fly us to Mamako Oosuki!"

"Whaaat? Don't be sillyyy. You're the one controlling iiiit."

"Huh? What are you talking about? You summoned this monster!"

"Ummmm, no, I didn't. I thought youuu did."

They stared at each other.

""......Uh?""

Then the giant beetle spread its wings and began furiously flapping them.

"W-wait! Then this monster isn't one of us?!"

"I gueeeess not?! Which meaaaaans..."

"Trouble! Aiiieee!"

And thus, a passing giant insect (not a monster at all) flew off toward the mountains with Amante and Sorella on board.

Meanwhile...

"Whew, we made it… Still, there was a whole lot of nothing on the way. Kinda disappointing…"

Masato's party had reached the coast.

The sandy beach traced a gentle arc. And beyond it, the sunlight's gleaming rays reflected off the ocean's surface. There was nothing but blue as far as the eye could see.

Below the coconut trees were coconut crabs, clinging to coconuts bigger than themselves and rolling them along.

It was the perfect beach.

"Whoa, the grains of sand are shaped like stars! Star sand!"

"We call it *Hoshizuna* in Japanese. The 'sand grains' are actually the fossilized corpses of protozoic creatures." *Grin.*

"Someone tell the resident blackhearted babe standing in the surf to a put a lid on it."

He begged for help preserving the emotion of the moment, but none came.

The girls were already hard at work developing the resort.

"How about we have a really long pier here, and cottages on the water at the end of it?" suggested Wise.

"That would be lovely! I've seen things like that in travel brochures, but never had a chance to go myself. How exciting! Hee-hee."

"I've never stayed anywhere like that! I'd really like to try!"

"Right, right? 'Kay, it's settled, then! Which means… Mamako!"

Wise and Porta snapped to attention, bowing. ""If you please!""

"You got it!" Their plea reached the doting mother nearby.

Mamako stood in the surf, placing her palms on the incoming waves.

"Mother Ocean… If you too are a mother, then surely you know how I feel… If we could vacation here, everyone would be so happy… So please, lend us your power."

Mamako's wish mingled with the water, washed away with the undertow, and drifted out to sea…or so they thought.

But suddenly the wave imbued with her wish was pulled beneath the ocean, vanishing.

"…Oh my?"

"Er…wait, what's up with that? What's going on?!" cried Wise.

"It looked like it got dragged under!" said Porta. "Eep! There's a hole down there!"

Wise and Medhi came splashing over and saw a pit yawning open in the shallows—one big and deep enough for a human to fall into.

Porta stared into the depths and saw something moving below.

"Eeeep! There's something down there! I-i-it's…!"

"What? What is it?"

"A monsterrrrr!" Porta shrieked, throwing her arms above her head.

A jet of water shot out of the pit. Wise and Porta were caught up in it and flung into the air.

"What the?!" "Eeeek!" "Wise! Porta!" Mamako reached out, but too late: They were tossed onto the beach…

"…Hmm? Gahhhh!!"

But fortunately, Wise and Porta landed on Masato. They were both unharmed, landing butt-first on the back of Masato's head and lower spine respectively.

"Ow! Geez, Masato, your head's as hard as a rock! It hurts to sit on!"

"It's not supposed to be sat on! Get your butt off my head!"

"Sorry, Masato! But that really helped!"

"Oh, sure, Porta, you can sit on me anytime. Think of my back as a cushion for a true lady."

Permission granted. "Don't mind if I do." "Then Mommy will, too!" "No, wait!" Medhi and Mamako also sat on Masato, and they all took a rest. Everyone except the human cushion was very soft and supple.

"Wait, this isn't the time to goof off! Masato, get up! There's a dangerous monster blocking our resort wish from reaching the sea!"

"Seriously? Say that first! Humph!"

Saying farewell to all the butts, Masato stood up…and beheld the monster.

A shellfish. The two halves of the shell were easily twice as wide as Masato was tall.

"What the heck is it? A clam? A cockle?"

"Hmm…it's really big, but I think it's a clam. I wonder how much miso soup we could make with it!"

"Ooh, clam in miso? That sounds delicious! Come on, everyone! Let's beat this thing and have a beachside miso soup party!"

No one heeded Wise's call.

"Wait, why isn't anyone shouting? Are you guys not into it?!"

"I dunno, miso soup just doesn't seem right...but I'm up for some seafood barbecue! Come on, people! Time to fight!"

Masato was totally ready to fill his belly with monster clam and nothing else.

Out of the corner of his eye, he saw Mamako and Porta whispering to each other.

Masato picked up a stick and charged. But it was a clam. A well-armored one, obviously.

No point in attacking the shell... In which case...

Watching his enemy's movements, he inched closer, and the moment the shell opened—"Now!"—he shoved the stick into the gap. It was your classic "poke it" plan.

"Hiding in your shell won't do you any good! I speak from experience! Take it from me!" Medhi yelled, following up with a stick poke of her own. The end of her stick was forked, and she wedged it in so the clam couldn't snap its shell closed.

The writhing edible part throbbed angrily...and then began to quiver.

"Ha! Look at it... Wise, you're up!"

"Huh? Me? Um, I can't use magic, so I've got no way to attack..."

The quivering monster clam unleashed a strange vibration! Masato was unaffected! Medhi was unaffected! Wise's magic was sealed!

"Great work again, Wise! You've fulfilled your quota of uselessness!" *Grin.*

"Nobody is better at getting their magic sealed than you!" *Grin.*

"Hey, assholes! This isn't funny!" *Grrrr!!*

Wise came after them in a violent rage, but Masato let Medhi handle this.

"We need a finisher... Were Mom and Porta planning something?"

They were on the beach behind him, making some sort of circle at their feet with bits of driftwood.

It seemed Masato had distracted the enemy long enough for them to finish.

"Yo, Porta! Mom! You ready to cook this thing?"

"Yes! Anytime!"

"Oh my! Ma-kun knows just what Mommy's thinking! I'm so glad!"

"Like mother, like child, I guess. Honestly, the second we started talking about eating it I kinda figured this was the plan. So..."

"Yes! Leave the rest to Mommy!"

Mamako stood in the surf and put her palms in the water.

"Mother Ocean... Can you give us a little spurt like this shellfish just did? Please?"

The ocean heard her call.

The water around the monster clam pulled back and then slammed in hard, rocketing the thing high over their hands, and it landed...

...right in the circle of wood.

Mamako turned and placed her palms on the sand.

"Mother Earth... My precious son and his friends want to have a beach barbecue. Lend me your power!"

A rumble deep inside the earth responded.

Underground magma rose up (super-localized), heating the crust above. Directly below the circle of wood. Which caught fire. Directly roasting the clam.

Now they just had to wait.

"In this world, it's eat or be eaten. Wham, bam, thank you, clam."

"Okay, everyone! Time for the barbecue!" Mamako called.

"Yay! This will be so much fun!" squealed Porta. "I'll watch closely and make sure the fire doesn't go out!"

"Skewers are the key to any real barbecue, but... Eh, this is close enough."

"Hee-hee. Don't sweat the small stuff, Ma-kun. Now, Mommy will finish her other job."

"Other job?"

Mamako shot a quick smile at the ongoing showdown between Berserk Wise and Medhi and then stepped into the surf once more, putting her hands in the water.

"Mother Ocean... I'm sorry for all these requests... But they're all for these precious children… Could you please give us a lovely cottage on the water?"

This time the wish was granted.

A long pier and cottages made of driftwood rose out of the ocean at one end of the beach. It was still soaking wet, but with the sun pouring down on it, it would dry in no time.

"And that's it for the first phase of our resort development! We have a private beach now!"

"That sure seemed simple… Are there *any* limits to Mom's powers?"

Masato looked from the pier to the cottages to Mamako's back, shaking his head…

And then he saw something else.

"…It happened with the earth, and now the ocean…," Mamako mumbled.

It wasn't anything major. Hardly worth staring at.

But he could see sweat rolling down Mamako's back.

Not just a single drop, either, but one drop after another.

I dunno if I've ever seen Mom sweat like that…not that I remember anyway.

She was sweating more than Masato, despite all the running around he'd done in that fight.

"…Eh, whatever."

The inviting scent of the sea's bounty over the fire was clearly more important.

Some time later…

"*Hahh…hahh…* We finally made it…"

"That beetle flew tooooo far! Did it really have to go all the way to the top of the highest mountaaain?! We had to climb back down and then cut through the jungle just to get here, and now I'm exhaaaausted! Boooo!"

"*I'm* the one who's tired! I was carrying you piggyback the whole time!"

"I mean…if we rode my tooooome, they'd see us comiiiing. Amante, you agreed this would be faaaaster."

"Yeah, I did! Argh, this is so unfair!"

Still carrying Sorella, Amante stepped onto the beach. They'd managed to keep their native islander disguises intact.

"Anyway, let's find Mamako Oosuki's party. They were headed toward the water, so…"

"Hmm… Where could they beee?"

They looked carefully around. Ocean. Beach.

Cottages on the water. A pier. A giant shell with steam rising off it.

"I don't remember those buildings… Also…"

"Ahhh! That claaaam! That's the guardian we placed heeeere!"

"You're right! Did Mamako Oosuki defeat it?! And eat it?!"

"I'm sure she diiiid! I bet it was deliiiicious! Arghh…that was our emergency proviiiisions!"

"Tch…and no signs of Mamako Oosuki and the kids… They had fun at the beach, ate, and moved on… Still…"

Amante frowned at the cottages and pier, thinking.

"This island should make it harder to use motherly powers…yet she went ahead and made all that? Without the Holy Swords, she shouldn't be able to summon the full force of the Earth and the Ocean…"

But she'd still managed it?

Was there no limit to Mamako's power?

"She is a constant source of terror… There isn't even any point explaining how terrified I am of her."

"Then doooon't… Anywaaay, if they're not here, we should look arooound."

"Yeah. I guess the traps we set against invaders didn't work?"

Sorella showed no signs of getting down, so Amante kept carrying her and headed over to the coconut trees.

At their bases, coconut crabs were rolling around coconuts several times their own size.

"This is the right place! They see this comical movement and get too close…"

"And the coconuts fall on their heeeads!"

"Yeah. But those are no ordinary coconuts…"

Both girls looked up just as two coconuts fell on them. There was a blinding light…

*   *   *

Ka-booom!

Masato thought he heard an explosion in the distance.

"Mm? Hmm... Was it just my imagination?"

They'd left the water cottages behind as they followed the coast around the island.

It was pretty noisy here; construction was in progress.

"Mother Earth...we'd like to make this road a little wider. If you don't mind..."

Mamako had her hands on the ground. The expansion of the jungle promenade began. The trees and shrubbery near the path moved sideways, the ground groaned, and stone tiles paved the open space.

There was now a broad road leading into the heart of the island.

"Whew... Wise, sweetie, how's that look?"

"Perfect! Just as planned. Having you around sure is a lifesaver!"

"Hee-hee. I'm glad to be useful. Next up is... Whoops!"

As Mamako stood up, she swayed, and Masato caught her.

"Uh, careful, Mom. Dizzy spell?"

"S-sorry, Ma-kun. I must have tripped."

"Nothing to apologize for, but... Wow, you're drenched in sweat."

"Yes, it's so humid! I'm sweating all over."

It was certainly a sultry jungle, but...this seemed excessive.

When he took his hands off her shoulders, his palms were soaking wet.

"...Uh, Mom?"

"Thank you, Ma-kun. Let's keep moving! What's next after the road?"

"Once we get a little farther back, we could make a hotel or a gift shop—something kinda resort-y, y'know? What do you think, Mamako?" asked Wise.

"That would be lovely! Let's do it."

"Great! Then let's get started! Go, go, go!"

"Go, go, go!"

"Go, go, *no*! Mom, you're... Ah, forget it."

Mamako was clearly in good spirits. The three of them pressed farther on.

Medhi and Porta were a good distance ahead, scouting.

"This is where the main road stops... So maybe we should have something here? Like a symbol of the island?"

"Yes! A fountain or...ooooh, a statue of Mama!"

"Great idea! A giant marble statue of this island's founder!"

Mamako would soon be looming over the center of the island.

The idea was enough to give Masato a headache.

"Hold it, you guys! Please, anything but that! Gimme this one thing!"

"You glance up, and there's your mother! No matter where you are on the island, you need only turn around, and she's waiting for you! Isn't that lovely?" *Grin.*

"Ha-ha-ha! That smile is downright diabolical! You've clearly proposed this just to torture me! I won't stand for it!"

"Well, Mamako. Hotels, shops, and a statue! When you're ready."

"A statue of me? Goodness, that's a little embarrassing...but I'll see what I can do!"

"Yo, don't even try!"

Masato reached out to stop her...

...but before he could, something grabbed him from the side.

"Mm? Is this...a vine?"

It was.

The vine was coiling around him like it had a mind of its own.

"Eep! M-Masato, this is bad! Look around us!" yelped Porta.

"Around—? Whoa! What is this?!"

There were vines all around them. Writhing like snakes, the color of poison, raising their "heads" at the party like cobras.

"What are these, monsters? Everyone, look out!"

"Vines...in a jungle...," said Wise. "Hold up, this could be real bad! Especially for cute girls like us!"

"They wrap around our limbs and hoist us in the air, squeezing... and as we groan in agony, they mockingly slip inside our clothing and... Oh! We can't let that happen!" cried Medhi.

"I'm a noncombatant, so... Eep! There's one after me!"

The vines were rubbing their leaves together as if mocking them, confirming their fears!

A moment later…

"Oh my! Eek!"

They all ensnared Mamako!

The self-proclaimed cute girls were unharmed.

"Mm, yeah, I was afraid of that… *Sigh*… Those things have no taste! Tch."

"I know it's an incredibly undesirable position to be in, but being snubbed doesn't really feel good either… They should understand how a maiden's mind works! Tch."

"Hey, you two! 'Maidens' don't stand around clicking their tongues at a time like this!"

"Mama's in real trouble!"

"They're so tight… Ahh!"

The narrow vines were wrapped around and around Mamako's hands and feet…around her chest and hips…pulling her off the ground.

"Oh my! Oh no!" Digging into places they really shouldn't. So tight Mamako couldn't move!

Mamako was in physical danger, but the greatest threat was to Masato's eyes. This was not something any son should have to see.

Yet, someone else was looking directly at her from the brush nearby. On the flowers and buds and stalks of the giant broccoli nearby were a great number of eyeballs, all staring avidly at Mamako's predicament.

"I never thought the forest itself would be a monster… Argh! Everyone, help me save Mom! We've gotta stop these vines!"

He hit one as hard as he could with a stick! "Ahh!" "Wah!" The vibrations traveled up the vines and made weird noises come out of Mamako.

"Crap, blunt-force attacks aren't working! All they're doing is creating aural disasters! Anybody have something that can cut vines?"

"Urgh… I'm so sorry… This is all because I lost my bag…"

"Porta, don't worry," said Medhi. "Let's just stay focused on helping Mamako."

"Yeah, Porta! Never fear! Even without her swords, Mom can… Oh! We can fix this with Mother Earth's power! Right, Mom?"

"I—I thought the same thing, and I've been asking, but…I can't reach!"

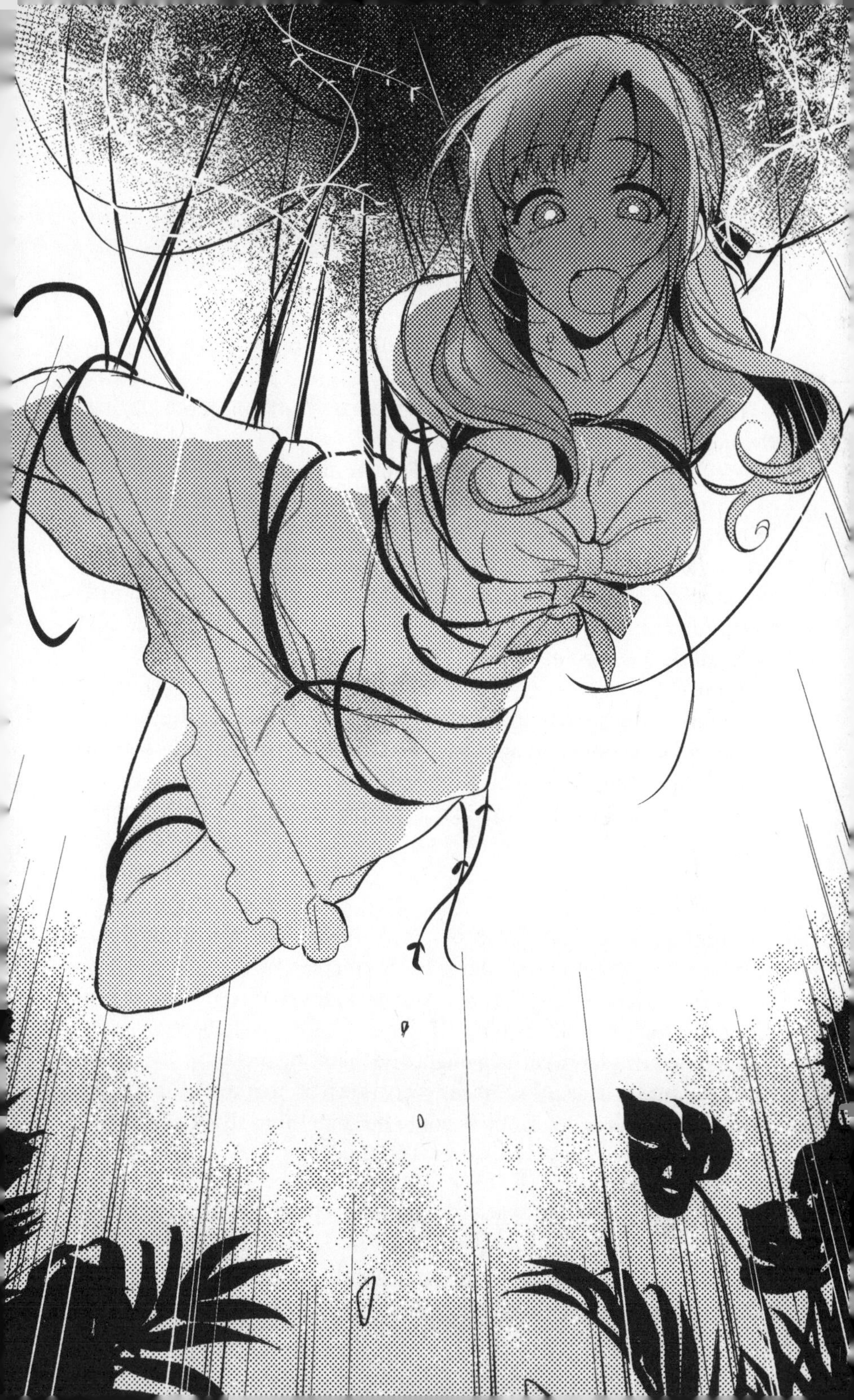

"You have to be touching the ground to do it? Then..."

Masato leaped on the nearest bunch of vines, pulling himself toward Mamako. They didn't really budge.

The girls followed suit, and everyone yanked.

"Here goes! Heave ho! Heave ho!"

"Heave ho! Y'know, I've been wondering... Why do we say *heave ho* when pulling things?" asked Wise.

"It's from old sailboats! They used to chant *heave ho* when raising the sails!"

"Wow, Medhi! You know so much! You're amazing!" said Porta.

"Well, with that question answered, let's pull!" shouted Masato. "Heave ho!"

Everyone pulled together, and Mamako slowly got closer to the ground. She managed to adjust her posture a bit, reached out toward the ground...

...and she touched it!

"Mom!"

"Right! ...Mother Earth...you'd be furious if anyone did this to you! These bad little boys and girls have tied me up in front of my son and his friends... They need to be punished!"

The fury of a mother (who's so not into being tied up) was activated!

Meanwhile...

"Arghhh! We got caught in our own traaap! You're so stuuuupid, Amante! I'm changing your name to Dumbanteeee!"

"You're the one suggested we take a look, Sorella! And I saved you from the trap, so quit griping! If it weren't for my Reflection skill, you'd have been screwed! You oughta be thanking me!"

"Sure, sure, thaaaanks. Aaaanyway, keep it moooving. Looook! They've made a rooooad. We've got to do something about Mamako's party quiiiick! Or they'll ruin everythiiiiing!"

"I know that! Geez!"

Wearing masks made of leaves, Amante and Sorella turned onto the newly paved jungle promenade.

The moved farther into the jungle, searching for their targets.

"Mamako Oosuki must have gone this way... Heh-heh-heh...that's perfect."

"Riiight? This leads to one of our best traaaaps."

"Yep. I don't need to explain what it is, but the plants back this way are all monsters, and they'll bully you so badly that you'll never want to come back to this island... Mm?"

Amante noticed the ground shaking and looked up to see what the commotion was...

Ahead of them, a giant broccoli stalk was swelling up. What looked like windows appeared on the surface—like an apartment complex.

Around it, daikon, carrots, and other giant root vegetables were growing, too, and becoming different kinds of shops.

Also...

"Huuuuh? Something's coming toward uuuus?!"

"That's..."

Jungle plants. Flowers, grass, vegetables, vines—a swarm of monster plants, furiously pumping their roots, stampeding toward them...or maybe running away from something?

Things were getting weird at the back of the stampede. The stragglers were getting pulled to the sides of the promenade and being transformed into fences woven from vines, flower-shaped streetlamps, street signs made from fruits, etc.

"She's using the monsters to make a rooooad!"

"Is this Mamako Oosuki's...? Wait, no time to think! We've gotta run!"

It was already too late. Amante and Sorella were getting caught up by the fleeing monsters.

A giant broccoli high-rise hotel, cottages made from other vegetables, each with pools of natural spring water for use by any guests.

Rows of fruit-shaped shops and facilities.

And a giant Mamako statue made of white marble.

The finishing touch.

"This! This is the resort we dreamed of!"

"From concept to completion in a matter of hours! Very impressive."

"I'm so happy! Yay! Yaaay!"

The girls were dancing with joy.

Meanwhile, Masato was shaking his head.

"Punishing monsters by turning them into building materials... That's beyond ridiculous, beyond impressive, beyond words."

He looked up at the glittering statue of Mamako and sighed.

But when he glanced at his mother...

...he found her sitting on the ground, breathing heavily.

"Hahh...hahh..."

"Wha...? M-Mom? You okay?"

"Hmm? Oh...yes, I'm fine, Ma-kun. Don't worry. Mommy's fine. See? Look, I feel great."

She flexed her slender arm, grinning.

That smile certainly looked like it always did, but there was a lot of sweat running down her face. With a few grunts, Mamako managed to get to her feet.

"Whew. And now the resort's finished!"

"Uh, yeah, well...seems that way. You satisfied now, girls?"

Guess not. Wise was happily yelling, "Mamako! Listen to this!" Her eyes were glittering. Apparently she'd had another idea.

"She's still going? Enough already. Mom's..."

...clearly tired. They should let her rest.

But she just patted Masato on the back, stopping him.

"Ma-kun, I'm fine. Don't you worry."

"You say that, but...I'm, you know..."

His feelings were simple enough.

I'm worried about her!

But actually admitting that was too much for him to put into words.

And in his strained silence, Mamako pushed past him.

"Ma-kun, Mommy feels certain she can do anything for you and your friends. The power just keeps coming! As long as you're with me, my mommy power is infinite."

"Don't be ridiculous... But, well, you've been ridiculous since the moment we set foot in this game."

"So don't you worry about letting Mommy dote on you. I'll dote on you aaall you like! Doing that makes Mommy happy. So really, don't worry about it."

She was saying it again. With a smile.

If she insists, then I guess it's fine?

He still wasn't sure. Part of him took her at her word, part of him didn't…

But the girls weren't giving him time to think. They were already gathered around.

"Whatcha talking about? Fill us in!"

"…Nothing. Never mind. What did you want?"

"Fine. Masato—ha, I mean Mamako!"

"Faking like you want something from me out of spite now, are we?"

"Yes, Wise? What is it?"

"You've built all kinds of shops, but what if we were the owners of these shops? What if we ran them ourselves? Wouldn't that be fun?"

"What kind of idiot runs a shop on an uninhabited island? There are no customers! …Ow!"

She'd stepped on his foot. Without even looking.

"This is a resort made by Mamako! Customers will show up any minute. So, Mamako, I want the clothes shop, Medhi'll take the cosmetics store, Porta the tropical juice stand, and that leaves you working as the hotel owner. What do you say?"

"Oh, that sounds lovely! This will be such fun! I'm in."

"Er…do I get a shop?"

"Great! That settles it! Which brings us to the next request…"

"Can we use your mom power to make everything the shops sell?" asked Medhi.

"If it's not too much trouble, could you do that? Please!" pleaded Porta.

"Hmm, well…" Mamako considered it. "Okay. I think I can handle everything we need. Hee-hee."

She agreed with a smile.

"Right! Then let phase two of the resort development begin!"

"""Yeah!"""

The girls were certainly getting themselves very worked up.

Not so much Masato.

"...I'm left out again." *Sulk.*

"W-we didn't mean to!" said Porta.

"Th-that's right, Ma-kun! That's not our intent! Right, Wise?"

"Of course not! We've got the perfect role for Masato."

"Oh yeah? What is it?"

"You have a grass skirt. This is an island paradise surrounded by beautiful ocean! There's only one thing for you to do. As the evening sky turns red, you'll provide the perfect entertainment... I'm talking...fire dance!" Fiyaaaa!

"My entire value is now in this grass skirt, huh?"

"That was just a joke," said Medhi. "I think it would be best if you do whatever you most want to do, Masato. Is there anything you've known was unachievable, but wanted so much it killed you inside?"

"What I want to do? Well..."

He looked at Medhi's smiling face, and it came to him.

"...survivalism?"

"Yes. Why not create a sort of attraction area that would allow just that?"

"Hmm..."

He could take over a section of the jungle and make it into a survivalist zone.

All that was required was to pick the location. He wouldn't need equipment or anything. That would just get in the way.

Which means I can do this without using Mom's power...or worrying about doing so.

And he could experience the blood-churning, skin-crawling, wildman life he'd dreamed of.

"...Not bad."

"*Not bad*? It's perfect for you! Admit it!"

"It's! Perfect! For! Me!"

"Good. That's settled. So first—"

"Gotta designate a survivalist zone! Where should it be...? There are no monsters left here, so that's boring... I'll go see if I can find a good spot! Be right back! Rahhhh!"

"Oh, wai— Masato?!"

He was off, in perfect running form, headed right down the promenade toward the coast.

Nothing was left in his mind but the survivalist life he'd been dreaming of and the face of his kindred spirit.

"Honing myself in the face of nature's harshest threats! Battles between men! Ohhh, this is gonna be great!"

Masato went blazing away.

Right past two island locals trapped in a vine fence, their behinds stuck in the air.

"Survivalist lifestyle, here I coooome!!"

Masato never even saw them.

"Sheesh, there he goes... What a dumbass."

"He must be very happy," said Medhi. "Good work, Wise."

"My! Were you the one who suggested the survivalist idea, Wise?"

"Er, well, um...I think it was Porta..."

"It wasn't me! It was Wise! She was thinking *so hard* about what would make Masato happeeeeagh?!"

"Portaaaa... Not. Another. Word. Got it?"

Porta's cheeks were twisted into silence.

Wise fanned her burning face, trying to cool them down. She got back in the driver's seat. "Okay, enough talk! Let's get to work. First—"

"What should I make? Tell me anything you like."

"Thanks, Mamako. But not yet... Before we start phase two, we need to find Porta's bag. We shouldn't overwork you any more than we have."

"Huh...?" Mamako looked surprised.

But all three girls lined up, bowing their heads.

"Sorry, Mamako. Really."

"Huh? Where'd this come from?"

"Using the power of the Earth without the Holy Sword is really exhausting, right?"

"When you finished this round of construction you were so worn out you couldn't even stand," said Medhi. "Even after the water cottages... We should have noticed then. Sorry."

"Th-that's not true! I'm fine..."

"You aren't fine! Mama, you always try too hard when you think it'll help Masato or us! We just want you to be honest with us!"

All three girls looked very serious.

Mamako gave up trying to smooth things over and smiled apologetically.

"Okay, yes. I'm definitely more tired than usual... How should I put it...? Normally it just takes a pinch, but now I have to put in several tablespoons!"

"Um, so...doing all this crazy stuff is basically the same as cooking to you?"

"But I don't think I'm feeling this way all because I don't have my swords. I certainly miss them, but...more than that...it's like I'm turning the flame up, but it just won't give me anything but the weakest flicker. Or like I'm turning the faucet and turning it, but only a trickle comes out."

"So something's clogging the works?"

"*Ha-choo!* Argh...well, at least my nose isn't clogged now. Thanks a lot, Medhi."

"Don't worry, Wise! I'll be delighted to put you out of your misery."

"Is there something jamming you?" asked Porta.

"Jamming me? Hmm... It does feel like there's something interfering with the entire process. I wonder if it's something about this island..."

Mamako suddenly looked up.

Her eyes fixed on a tall mountain in the distance.

"But it isn't very clear to me...so I'll just accept your feelings gladly and say that getting our equipment back seems like a very good idea. We can start phase two after that."

"Okay, cool! Then let's go find Porta's bag."

"Which means finding where we landed," said Medhi. "Where was it...? I don't think it was all that far from the jungle cottage, but—"

"Guess we should head back there first, then?"

"Yes!" agreed Porta. "But if we try to force our way through the jungle, we'll get lost!"

"That's right. Safety first," said Mamako. "Let's go! Onward!"

The party set off, moving away from the island shopping district and down the promenade.

As they walked, they kept chatting—something any lady has a knack for.

"Still, you surprised me, Wise... Hee-hee."

"Uh, Mamako? What're you laughing about? What did I do?"

"You really thought hard about Ma-kun. I was so glad to hear that! Hee-hee."

"We're back on this again?! Enough! I did think about it, just...not for *that* reason!"

"I would welcome you with open arms. You pass the mom test! Hmm...I suppose we'd need a bigger house if you were going to move in with us."

"You're planning on living there, too?! Wait, I guess if it's Mamako I'd actually prefer that..."

"If that's a benefit, I'd like to put myself forth as a candidate. If you'll have me."

"I want to live with Mama, too!"

"My, my! Then, Medhi and Porta can all live in the same house with us! We'll figure out which of you will marry Ma-kun later. Hee-hee."

"Flawless housekeeping, unrivaled in combat, the ultimate mother— living with her is the real objective, and Masato just a bonus... That's been his destiny all along, huh? ...Hang in there, Masato."

The hero had a harsh road ahead of him, and Wise offered up a silent prayer on his behalf...

But just then.

"...Hm? What's that?"

Wise noticed something sticking out of the vine fence on the side of the road.

Two round things, covered in a sort of rind, with a crack running down the middle.

"Some kind of peach? ...It's awfully big for a peach...and not quite the right shape..."

"Is something the matter? Wait... Those are..."

Medhi stepped over, inspecting them up close.

Then she tried pinching them. "Oh, they're soft!" "Quite soft."
Pinches. Squeezes. Quite resilient!

""Eeeek?!""

The peaches let out some weird, alluring squeaks. Wait...

"Mmphh! Mmmphh mmph mutt! Mmmph-mmphmmp mmmphh!"

"Mmmphhhhhhh. Mmmph mmmmph-mmph mmphhhh!"

"Huh? Talking peaches? ...Wait... Do those voices sound familiar?"

"Wise! They do! Look here!"

They peered over the fence and found two upper bodies, bound
tightly. And two familiar faces...

Amante and Sorella, with gags made of vines.

"The Heavenly Kings of the Libere Rebellion?! Why are you guys
here?! ...And how the heck did you end up like this?!"

"Clearly, this is how they get their kicks."

""Mmphh-mmmphmmphh!""

"Wise! Medhi! What's—eep?!"

"Oh my! Amante and Sorella!"

""Mmmm?!""

The moment they saw Mamako, both faces stiffened.

Meanwhile...

"I don't get it...but this is our chance, right?" Wise grinned.

"The perfect opportunity. They're positioned right where we need
them." Medhi grinned back.

Their smiles growing even more malicious, they picked up two
sticks and took some practice swings. *Vvvp! Vvvp!* ""Mmmphhhhhhh!!" It seemed that the Heavenly Kings' asses were doomed...

But instead...

"No need to punish them. I'll handle that."

...A cold voice came from the brush across the fence. A small figure
stepped out.

It was wearing an oversize coat, black as a shadow, yet the short hair
was a dull white. The figure had a dazed look about the eyes.

Its face and voice were both cute, like a girl's...

Then, multiple skeleton soldiers emerged, grabbing Amante and Sorella. ""Mmmmppphhhphhh?!"" They yanked on the two girls and started to drag them away into the jungle.

"This is part of their punishment. Don't hold back. Pull tighter so the vines strangle them."

""Mmph?! Mmm-mm-mmph-mmppphhh!""

"W-wait a moment! That looks painful! You should be a little nicer…!" Mamako ran toward the fence.

But a tiny palm thrust out in her direction.

"You're Mamako Oosuki? Consider this my way of saying hello."

The palm pushed into Mamako's belly.

"Er……?!"

Mamako was sent flying backward over the fence behind her and into the jungle beyond.

A single blow—not even a blow, just a gentle push. But it had easily launched her—launched *Mamako*.

Wise, Medhi, and Porta had all seen it happen, witnessed it with their own eyes, yet could not comprehend it. They were left speechless. Too stunned to even breathe.

"Is that all? No—is this merely what you are without your equipment? Then there is no need to fight you further. We shall meet again."

And with that, the interloper vanished into the brush, following the skeletons as they dragged Amante and Sorella away.

Long after they'd vanished, long after their footsteps had faded from earshot…

…the girls finally snapped out of it.

"Wh…what was that?!"

"I saw the Libere mark on his back… There's a third one?! N-no, before we worry about him…"

"Mama! Mamaaaa!"

They scrambled into the jungle to see if Mamako was all right.

"……Okay, here's far enough. Ditch these idiots and get back to the lair."

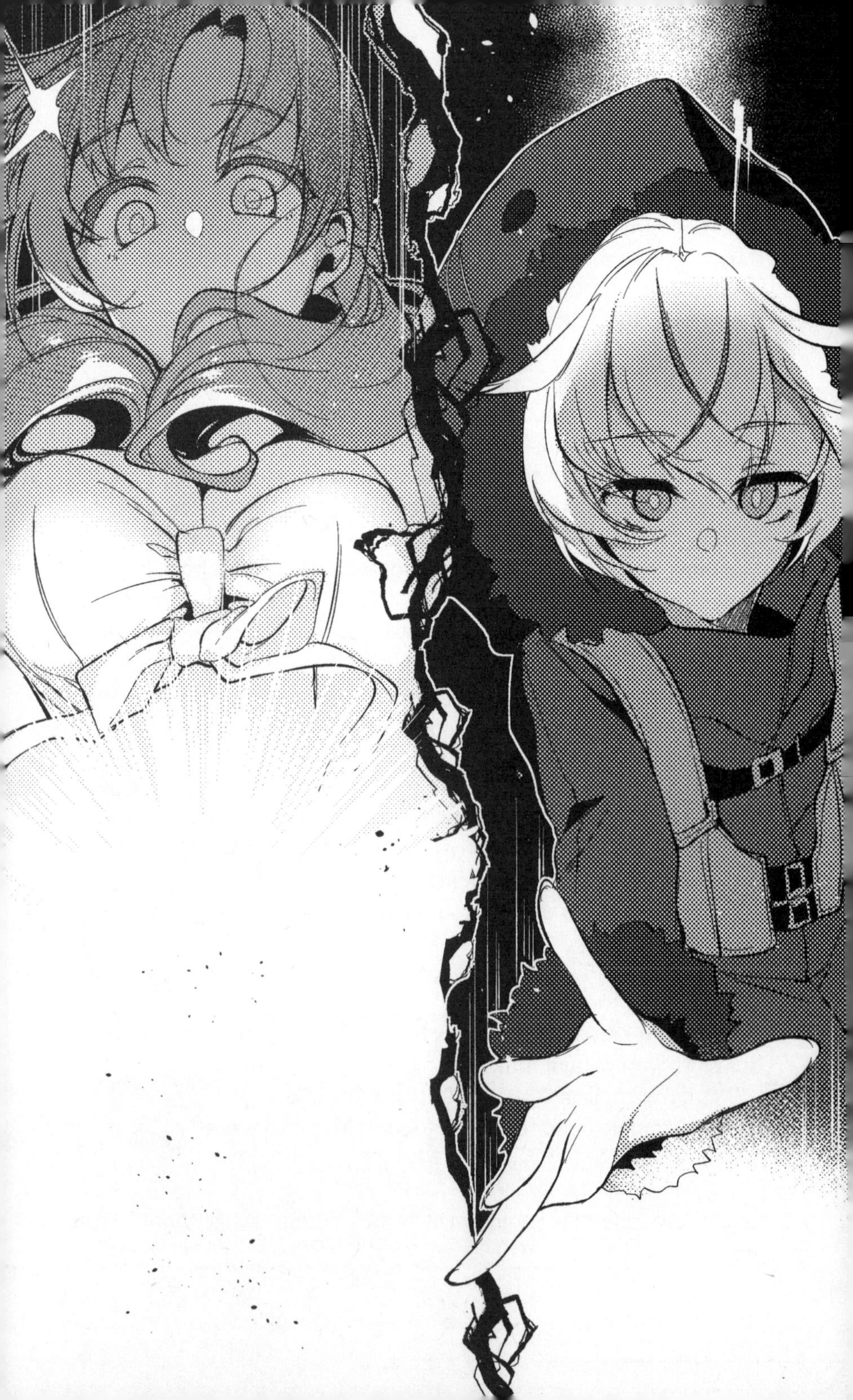

The skeletons obeyed his order. "Mmph?!" "Mmph!!" Amante and Sorella were flung onto the jungle floor as the skeletal minions stalked away.

Furious at this treatment, Amante and Sorella managed to gnaw through their gags and glare up at their tormentor.

"Fratello! Who do you think we are?! Treat your cohorts better!"

"Every part of me huuuurts! If this leaves any scaaars, it's your faaault! You'd better make it up to meee!"

"Shut up, you incompetent clowns."

"How rude! We aren't—!"

"Did you drive Mamako Oosuki off the island according to the plans we laid yesterday?"

"Uhhhh… Weeeell…that didn't work ouuut."

"You got trapped in some vines in a very undignified position AND they found out your identities… What else could it be but incompetence?! Tell me that, you useless idiots."

"Ack…"

"Urrrrgh…"

He gave them a cold, listless glare. Neither could argue that he had a point.

"You women are so stupid and incompetent… It makes me want to puke."

Fratello was done looking at them. He turned toward the jungle.

"Change of plans. Amante, Sorella, use your stupid strength and undead army to locate Porta's bag. They already know you're on the island. No need to be choosy about your methods. Make sure you get it first."

"Boooo! We're all beat up and you want us to wooork? Is this a jungle or a sweaaaatshop?!"

"What're you gonna do with the bag, anyway?!"

"Give it back to Mamako Oosuki. Once she's in peak condition, I'll fight her fair and square, and I'll win."

"Er…w-wait, are you insane?!"

"This is Mamako we're talking abouuut! If you have to fiiiight, do it now, before she gets her equipment baaaack! This is our chaaaance!"

"Not a problem."

Fratello looked down at his hands, tightening his grip.

"Y'all..."

""*Y'all*?!""

"Ahem... I possess immense power—power that enables me to blow away the strongest mother one-handed. I am one of the Libere Rebellion's Four Heavenly Kings, the one who threatens the power of mothers—and Mamako Oosuki ain't no threat to Frighten-Mom Fratello, ya hear?!"

""*Ya hear*?!""

"Ahem."

The lone wolf named Fratello stalked off, his expression blank.

"I'll monitor their base. If you locate the bag, bring it to me. Understood?"

"Wait one minute! You don't get to boss us around!"

"Just because you're a little strong doesn't give you the riiiight! Fratelloooo! I hope you get caught in a jungle trap and sufferrrr!"

"Humph. Unlike you, I'm not stupid enough to get caught in the traps we set. I'm not that stupid!"

He repeated the most important part of his statement a second time and promptly vanished into the jungle.

The Hero Masato Oosuki's Ultimate Move Development 2

With ultimate moves, you usually have to, like, release the hidden power lying dormant within yourself, right? ...Hnggg...hngggggggg!!

MEDHI

I hear the strangest noise... Oh, it was Masato. Training again?

It wasn't *that* strange, but moving on... Nice timing, Medhi. I figured you're the best person to ask about this stuff.

MEDHI

I certainly know a thing or two about drawing on the forces within... Unleashing one's pent-up emotions...

Uhhh, never mind. I'm not trying to be a dark-sided hero here...

MEDHI

You think I'm trying to tempt you over to the dark side? I'm hurt... Grrrrrrr...

Stop unleashing your dark power on me, would ya?!

Chapter 3 The Incident Occurred While I Was Gone. I Knew Then I Was Never Meant to Be a Detective.

The morning sun rose above the horizon, illuminating the water cottages.

Blinding sunbeams streamed in through the windows, bathing Masato's face and forcing him awake.

"Ugh...morning? *Yawn...* Wait."

He turned away from the light and looked around, dazed.

This was a bedroom. Not that large of a room—yet it had five beds, all squeezed in here together. Each one had an exotic canopy draped over it, so this place totally screamed "resort," but that only added to the cramped feel.

But there was only Masato here, which alleviated that a bit.

"Everyone else already woke up? Hold on..."

He could hear a tapping sound, like someone chopping food.

"...Geez, I told her not to cook for me!"

Masato quickly changed from his pajamas into a Hawaiian shirt and shorts, and ran out of the bedroom.

The water cottages weren't particularly roomy. The bedroom door led directly into the living room, a space for relaxing on shell-shaped couches.

The kitchen was located on the side of the room, where Masato spied the back of the person he needed to talk to:

Mamako, humming to herself as she got breakfast ready.

"Mom! We need to talk."

"Oh, Ma-kun! Good morning! You're up early. As a reward for waking up on your own, let me give you a good-boy head rub!"

"That's great and all, but I'm not in the mood for goofing around!"

He almost started yelling at her.

But he stopped himself in time, took a deep breath, and spoke calmly.

"Yesterday you ran into the Libere Heavenly Kings, and one of them knocked you down pretty hard, right? You sure you're okay to move around?"

"Oh my! Thank you for worrying. But I'm fine."

"I really can't trust those words from you, not at a time like this…"

"But I really am fine! It wasn't like he hit me hard. He just gave me a little push backward!"

"So it was just a knockback attack? Still…"

Mamako getting thrown at all was cause for alarm.

And not just that—without their equipment, they couldn't use any healing spells, didn't have any healing items, and didn't have the materials to create any. There was nothing they could do if someone got hurt. Yet, Mamako was getting up early and making breakfast just like always.

"Hee-hee. You're worried about your Mommy, Ma-kun?"

"W-well…I guess. Sort of."

"Then it's up to Mommy to make sure her precious son doesn't have to worry. Ma-kun, would you kneel for me?"

"Huh? Uh, sure…"

He did as he was told, kneeling on the floor.

Mamako put her arms around his head, pulling his ear against her stomach.

"…Uh."

"Now, Ma-kun. Listen close. Is Mommy's belly saying, 'Ouchie!' where it got hit?"

"Of course not. Bellies can't talk. Duh. This is so dumb."

"Then Mommy is just fine. No problems at all."

"Rrgh…"

She was totally treating him like a child, comforting him, and that was so frustrating, but at the same time…

A mother's belly, the first home (biologically speaking) that he'd known—it was impossible not to get a sense of relief from it, impossible not to find himself calming down. It was soft and warm, and it drained the tension from him. This was also frustrating, but…

Masato gently pushed Mamako back and stood up.

"…Guess I'll have to take your word for it."

"Thank you. I'm glad to hear it."

"But don't push yourself, okay? If anything feels off, tell me. I'm not like you. I'm not magically good at *everything*, but someday I'll get my hands on true strength! I'll have power even greater than yours! Hopefully!"

"I know. I'm looking forward to it! Hee-hee."

"Just you wait! My evolution will be worth it."

When this would happen was a mystery, but he had faith.

"In that case, Ma-kun, there is one favor I'd like to ask."

"Oh? What is it?! Lay it on me!"

"Could you go track down Wise, Medhi, and Porta? The three of them went out for a morning walk, but breakfast is almost ready. Let's get everyone back together and eat!"

"My first job, and I'm already an errand boy…"

Every journey begins with a single step. Masato decided this was his.

Masato left the cottage and went down the long pier.

He was aiming for a relaxing stroll, but it was hard to feel relaxed.

"I can't believe anyone could blow *my* mom away single-handedly… Medhi said they might be a third Heavenly King? If I'd been there—"

Even in jest, he couldn't bring himself to pretend he could have made a difference.

"*Sigh*… Blue skies, blue sea, white sand…a flawless resort. And yet the mission this hero's been given is a fetch quest. That's my reality. Argh, if only I had a power that could astonish everyone…"

It was like he was in paradise, but there was a cloud over his head alone.

He reached the beach.

"Gotta find the girls, or we can't eat. Better get looking… Heeeey! Breakfast's ready! Gather round!" he called.

No answer.

No sign of anyone in the water, on the beach, or in the jungle. Just some weirdly burnt-looking coconut trees and coconuts...

And a big burnt peach.

"...Mm? A peach? Here? And why is it burnt?"

Round, with some sort of rind on it, a faint groove down the center...definitely peach-like.

There was an unnatural outcropping of vines at the jungle's edge, and the peach was growing out of it...or maybe just jutting out of it?

Either way.

"This might make for a good dessert after breakfast. I'd better pick it."

He grabbed the round sides with both hands. "Whoa, that's really soft! Don't wanna squish it." He flexed his fingers, enjoying the sensation a bit as he carefully pulled...

"Mahh?!"

There came a familiar, dazed-sounding voice.

"Wait, I know that voice... Fratello?"

"That you, sonny? Those your hands on my tush?"

"Wait, this isn't a peach? Your...tush? This is a butt? *Your* butt?!"

"Like I said, that's my tush. Let go of it, will ya?"

"R-right! Sorry!"

Fratello seemed super-calm, but Masato hastily let go anyway.

"Good grief... I took one step into the jungle, and these dang vine monsters swiped all my clothing... I made myself some clothes out of plants and came here, then got caught in a trap we set... How stupid is that, eh?"

"Huh? A trap *we* set?"

"Never mind that. Could ya help me out here, sonny? I'd owe you one."

"Will do. I'll make sure you pay me back, though!"

Masato got right on it. He grabbed Fratello's waist and gave him a good, hard pull. "Mwgahhhhh!" "Those vines are pretty tight, huh?" Fratello was letting out some weird moans. They didn't sound right.

Masato switched tactics, trying to rip the vines directly. He slowly managed to free the body, the delicate limbs, and finally the leaf-covered white head.

"I should be able to pull you out now... Here goes. One, two... Whoa!"

"Mah!"

He grabbed Fratello from behind and pulled hard. The boy came out far more easily than anticipated, and Masato fell backward with Fratello on top of him.

Fratello ended up straddling Masato's belly, swaying a bit, staring blearily down at him.

"Whew... Ya really bailed me out there, sonny."

"You're welcome. Wow, you're light... Are you getting enough to eat?"

"Darn tootin' I am! Just can't seem to put on much muscle... Wonder why."

"Well, no use asking me. I dunno. Just the way you were made, I guess."

Not really thinking about it, Masato gave Fratello's body a few quick prods. Definitely barely any muscle. Shoulders, arms, around the waist, legs—no flab, but no muscle, either.

...Kinda like Porta's build.

Naturally, he'd never been *this* handsy with Porta, but she and Fratello had similar builds, or at least bone structures.

Then Fratello suddenly hopped up. "Guh!" "Sorry, kid." He stepped off Masato's belly.

"Anyhoo, since we're both here, I'd love to trade blows like male friends do, but...*yawn*...I spent all night trapped in them vines, so I'm plumb tuckered out. Gotta bid ya farewell for now."

"You should. And take a bath—you smell like leaves. Do you have a bath? If not, you can borrow ours..."

"That'd make two things I owe ya, sonny. Can't have that."

"Don't see the point in standing on that principle, but suit yourself."

"Principles make the man, sonny. Next time we meet, I'll be sure to pay ya back for this favor. Bye!"

"Sure. See you later."

Fratello ran off into the jungle.

He'd been sort of hoping to spar some more, so it was a shame to see him leave, but Masato let him go…

And then the girls came running down the beach, clearly excited.

"Oh, Masato!" shouted Wise. "Perfect timing! Listen!"

"Where'd you guys come from? I was just looking for you, and—"

"Never mind that! Listen to us first!" said Medhi. "There are people on the island!"

"People are working in the hotel and the shops!" cried Porta. "They're carrying luggage in! It's like a real resort now!"

"…Wait, seriously?"

After a quick meal, the party left the water cottages.

Even as they moved down the pier, the island's transformation was obvious.

There were a number of airships in the sky. Several large sailing ships were anchored in the shallows. Dinghies lowered at their sides, filled with people. Merfolk were towing those dinghies to the shore.

And beastkin laden with luggage were piling out of the dinghies and out of the airships above, descending on the island.

"Oh my! So many tourists! Business will be booming!"

"Too much booming, too fast…"

The party joined the flow of tourists, heading down the promenade.

So many people. Not just tourists, but people acting as guides. "This way, please!" "Please don't eat the wild fruits!" They were clearly working hard and making a good impression, but…

The party soldiered on before finally reaching the shopping district, which was even more crowded.

There were people at each of the fruit-shaped shops and vendors, at the root vegetable cottages, and at all windows of the broccoli high-rise hotel.

"Yikes… So many people, so many ears and tails…"

"And people working in the lodgings and the shops, all open for business… This really did become a resort overnight."

"Did Mama push herself again?"

"What could this mean? …Oh, I know! You ladies were so nice

to Mommy, and such good girls, that the mom power granted our wishes! I'm sure that's what this was. Hee-hee."

"That's a load of nonsense. You totally asked for this on the sly, right, Mom? …Wait."

Masato spotted someone.

A beastkin woman was staring up at the Mamako statue. Black pointy ears, a long thin tail, black hair.

A cat woman, wearing a summer-style nun habit (with a bit more skin exposed).

"A nun habit… This sinking feeling in my chest… Nope, didn't see a thing. Nothing to see here."

Masato was about to drag his eyes away…

…when the woman abruptly died and became enveloped in a coffin.

"Geez…"

"Give it up, Masato. This is our destiny. Only one person has such improbable deaths and coffin exposure."

"Argh, that's *exactly* why I was trying to avoid her!"

Mamako obtained a revival item from a friendly tourist in exchange for an autograph.

They used it to bring the coffin's occupant back to life—it was definitely her. Even before the coffin had entirely faded, unflappable eyes were staring right at them.

"…Hi, Shiraaase."

"We meowt again. For reviving meow once again, I meowst express my gratitude."

"You're already really forcing the cat talk. If you're gonna be a cat girl, just lazily stick a *meow* at the end of every sentence, please."

"Following the established template is, of course, invaluable, but Shiraaase—er, Meowraaase—believes it is equally imeowportant to investigate mew purrssibilities. I can infooormeow you of this!"

"You really need to stop changing your name on a whim."

"Meownever."

She was going to be the mysterious cat-pun nun until she got sick of it, apparently.

"Right, Meowraaase, what made you come all the way meowt here?"

"You mean, what brings meow to the Aichi server? The answer is meowst simple. I exist meownly to ensure that you all have a purrleasant and enjoyable game life. Even if you meowsied into the depths of mewhell itself, I would find you all and come scampering. That is meow job."

"I feel like you're generally more of a threat to our safety and enjoyment...and there's no respite, even in the bowels of hell. Or mewhell, whatever that is. Is it this situation we're in right now?"

"Wherever you may go, your own meowther, your purrty, and other people's meowther's will follow. The purrfect adventure! Meow-ha-ha."

Meowraaase mockingly patted Masato's shoulder with a paw.

She then turned to Mamako.

"Ms. Meowraaase, those ears and tail are simply meowvelous! Hee-hee."

"Well, this is as close to a vacation as I'meow likely to get! I'meow trying to have a little fun. But meow did you all end up here? This island was left off the map purr a reason."

"We were supposed to be headed directly to an island south of Meowterville for a vacation, but—"

"Meowr airship crashed on the way, stranding us here. It was like, *whoosh, ka-boom*," said Wise. "Plus we lost all meowr gear and had to start meowr survivalist life literally naked."

"But thanks to Mamako, we had everything we mewded," explained Medhi. "So we decided to develop our own meowsort and vacation here!"

"And when we came to check it out, we found Shiraaase! I mean, Meowraaase!" added Porta.

"Yo, people. No need to talk the way she is. That'll just encourage her."

"Meowat's meowot meowrue."

"SEE?! Now I can't even figure out what's she saying! Please don't add fuel to the fire."

"Okay, okay," said Wise, giving in. "But, uh, in the bad news department, Amante and Sorella are on the island."

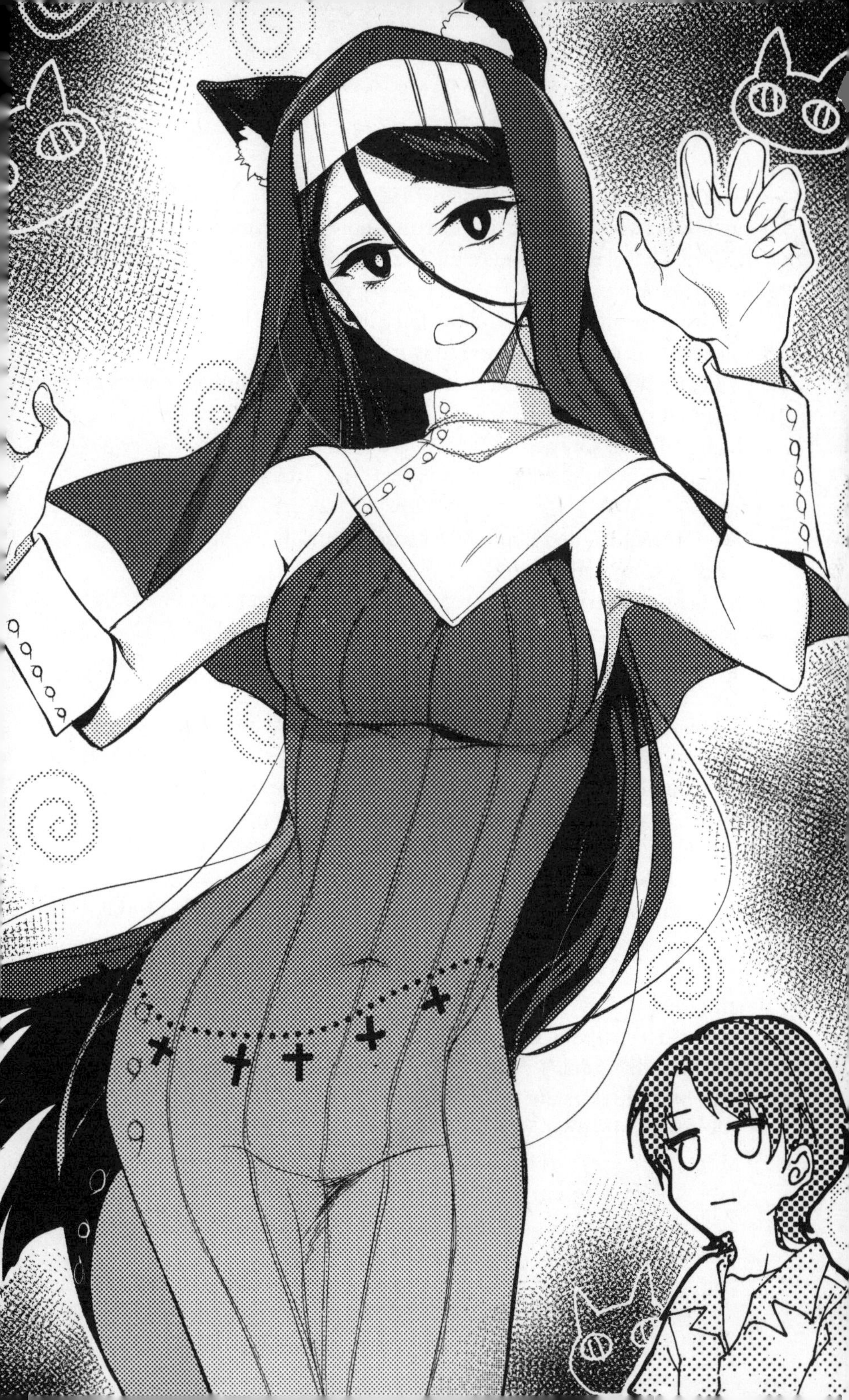

"And not just them," continued Medhi. "There's a third Heavenly King. It was over so fast we don't really know much yet…"

"Curious. I feel well versed in meowst of the situation. Thank you for infooormeowing me of this. For meow part…"

Meowraaase glanced around the party, took a long look at Porta and her lack of bag, and then appeared worried.

"…I can infooormeow you that the loss of your equipment comes as the meowst significant shock."

"Eep…I-I'm so sorry…"

"It's not your fault, Porta," said Wise. "The situation left us with no options."

"We were all excited about the vacation and thoughtlessly let our best gear go," agreed Medhi.

"I have meow intention of rebuking you for what happened. But since it has…I do worry that it will throw a paw in my plan."

Meowraaase thought hard for a minute.

"Your plan? …Oh, right, of course you have one."

"Allow meow to be honest. I do. When I used my meowdmin purr-ivileges to determine your location, I thought the meowse trap had sprung, but without your equipment…Wise and Medhi can't even use meowgic!"

"Sad, but true."

"Especially for me. Wise is obviously no different from—ow!"

"Oh, sorry about that, Medhi! Your foot seemed like it was just begging me to stomp on it!" *Stomp, stomp.*

"And we can't rely on Purrta's items, either. Meowsato never was much of a fighter…"

"Ack…that's…that's not true! I could technically fight before! Just not without my gear…"

"And Meowmako's out of commission, too."

"Oh? I'm totally fine. Even without the swords, I've managed to—"

"Mom, stop. We're not allowing it."

Wise, Medhi, and Porta all nodded in agreement. No more forcing herself.

"That certainly could be cat-astrophic."

"You know, with you talking like that, it's impossible to take you seriously…but you're right. Unfortunately, it doesn't feel like we'll be very useful…"

"No, no, of course you will, meow. I just feel sorry for you getting meowxed up in all this without your equipmeownt," said Meowraaase without even batting an eye.

Everyone else turned pale.

"Uh, crap! We've gotta find our equipment, stat! This is bad!"

"Find the bag before trouble finds us!"

"Hurry! We don't have a second to spare!"

"I'll do my very very best!"

"Okay, let's split up! I'll go—"

"I think we should first ask around and see if anyone picked it up for us. The jungle's dangerous, so let's not go in there alone, okay? Promise Mommy."

"Uh, right, right, sure! Commence searching!"

They scattered in all directions.

But as much as they wanted to hurry, the area was jam-packed with tourists. The simplest movements took ages, involving many bumped shoulders, apologies, and further bumps the moment they turned around.

And they were being watched.

"The island we wanted to remain uninhabited ended up with lots of people on it, which is bad…"

"But maybe not all baaaad."

They were lounging in a tropical café, elegantly sipping on tropical juice.

Amante wore a tiger-striped Hawaiian shirt, while Sorella had found one with bones on it. Both pairs of eyes were on Masato's party.

"Like hiding trees in a forest—with all these people around, we can sit right here, and no one will notice."

"And instead of working up a sweaaaat, we can relaaaax and still monitor them just fiiiine. This is greaaaat."

"Wetting our whistles with one hundred percent juice, watching them with one hundred percent no wasted effort…this is pretty nice, really."

Amante moved the bag from her feet to the table.

It was a shoulder bag. There was a bunny doll hanging off of it, swaying forlornly.

"They're running around searching for Porta's bag, unaware we found it first! Mwa-ha-ha! This is hilarious."

"They're soooo duuumb. It's hilaaaarious! Ahhh-ha-haa... Soooo... now whaaat? Do we do as Fratello saaaid? Should we give it baaack?"

"Hell no. No reason we should follow Fratello's orders. I wanna do something to teach these people a lesson. Especially Wise the Sage and Medhi the Cleric. I wanna teach them a couple lessons each."

"I agreeee. We have to pay them back for yesterdaaaay. Hmm...but let's think about it laaater. First, we need to celebrate being ahead of Mamakoooo."

"Yep. A toast to victory! Heh-heh. Mwa-ha-ha!"

They clinked their glasses together, laughing merrily.

But they were being watched.

"Mind if I ask mew one question? Purrdon the intrusion."

"What? We already paid for the juice."

"I'meow not here for the bill. About what mew just said...the bag on the table belongs to the Traveling Merchant Porta? You're purrsative?"

"Of course we are. Only the owner can open it, so we can't check the contents, but I've seen this doll before. Wait—"

"Why would a waitress ask thaaat? None of your busineeeeess. And whyyyy are you talking so weird?"

Annoyed, they turned around...

...and found Meowraaase staring silently at them.

"Huh? ...Oh...y-you're the admin?!"

"Purrease remain quiet. Meowmako and her purrty are still close by. If mew raise a fuss, they'll notice."

"Th-that would be baaad! I don't want to fiiiight. Let's be quieeet!"

"Thank mew very meowch. Now..."

Keeping her eyes locked on the two tense girls, Meowraaase considered her next move.

What meowxactly is going on here?

Meowraaase had been planning on filing a situation report with management while Mamako and company searched for the bag, but the moment she stepped into the café to do so, she'd found two Libere Heavenly Kings sitting there.

And the bag the party was looking for was with them. Far too convenient.

I'd love to brag about this to Meowsato's purrty and play cat and meowse with them about it, but…this is quite a purrdicament.

The two girls staring wordlessly up at her seemed to be in even more of a predicament, however. What was her next move?

Either way, she had to recover the bag.

But I'meow a noncombatant. Even without fighting, I'm meowst likely to die here…

In which case, getting word to Mamako took top priority.

Right meow they're missing their equipment. And with the crowds around us here…purroblematic.

She had to avoid any kind of fighting. But how?

For now, she chugged the two glasses of tropical juice on the table. "Hey! Those were ours!" "Aaaaah!" That gave her a moment to think.

"…Enough playing around."

Meowraaase removed her cat equipment.

She put the cat ear headband on Amante's head and the cat tail accessory on Sorella's head…

"Amante, Sorella…what say you team up with me?"

…and proposed a betrayal.

Meanwhile:

Masato had immediately broken his promise to his mother and headed out on his own.

"That bag is definitely still in the jungle. The area where we landed was designated a survivalist zone… Not many people would be interested in such a harsh environment. Instead of asking around, searching for ourselves will be way more…"

…*efficient*, he thought.

"Darling, if we hollowed out this tree and made it a house, wouldn't it be lovely?"

"Yes, honey. But let's not rule out living in a cave."

"Daaad! Mooom! This is like the mountain behind our house!"

"Ha-ha-ha! What are you saying, son? This is far milder than that!"

"There aren't even any carnivores! It's so safe here. Barely worth calling a jungle."

The survivalist zone was already packed with tourists.

And given the high physical stats beastkin had, what was a harsh natural environment to a human was basically just a playground to them. "Ah-ahhh-ahhhhhh!" "Yee-haw!" Adults and children alike were swinging around on vines like Tarzan.

"Ready...go!"

""""Uraghhhhhh!"""""

There were groups using their sharp claws to race each other to the tops of slick broccoli stalks.

This was more of an athletics zone now. And one on easy mode.

"Uh...maybe it *would* be faster to ask people in the shopping area if they were coming back from playing in the jungle..."

Masato was starting to regret his decision.

Then he noticed all the beastkin around him moving. Every ear twitched, all turning in the same direction. Toward the water.

"...Um, what is it?"

"Just heard a loud honking sound. And then...yeah, an announcement for some sort of event."

"R-really? I didn't hear anything..."

But the beastkin clearly had. "Wanna go?" "Yeah." "Let's!" Gathering the people around them, they started heading toward the sound.

What should Masato do?

"Hmm...I've gotta find the bag, but...I *am* curious..."

Maybe just a peek. He followed the others to check it out.

When he left the jungle, he found...

...a rectangle drawn on the white sand with a stick.

It was divided evenly into two sections, with a net set up in the middle—all ready to go.

Once a sizable crowd had appeared, Shiraaase stepped forward in a black bikini.

"We will now begin the uninhabited island beach volleyball event!"

No sooner had the words left her mouth than the crowd erupted in cheers. "That's what I've been waiting for!" "Hell yeah!" "You're hot!" "Yet, I'm already a mother! Heh-heh-heh!" Shiraaase seemed quite pleased.

Before the match could begin, there were announcements to be made. Shiraaase took the referee's seat and infooormed the crowd.

"The beach volleyball match is about to begin! This match is being held with the cooperation of a certain organization, so one team will be composed of members from said organization. There will be only one set. Whichever team scores fifteen points first will be the winner."

The crowd seemed to be clamoring for more than that, but to no avail.

Other voices were shouting for girls in swimsuits, and they got their wish.

"Then let's introduce this organization's team! Come on down!"

Shiraaase looked to the air above the court on the right. Floating above it...

...was a tatami-sized magic tome. Two girls jumped down, one carrying the other on her shoulders...

Thump! Amante and Sorella landed in the middle of the court.

"Ha-ha! Nailed it."

"Hiiii! Cheer for uuuus."

Both were wearing two-piece Rebellion uniforms. Bodies that had always been in great shape looked even more fit in this sporty gear. Judging by their outfits, it was easy to see they meant business.

"Next, let's introduce our challengers! Come on out!"

Shiraaase gestured toward the crowd, which parted, allowing two girls to step out, shoulder to shoulder.

"Geez, one word from Shiraaase and look what we have to do. I'm in, of course, but still."

On the right, we have Wise, wearing a ravishing crimson bikini, and doing a few light stretches.

"I have no complaints about the match itself, but I am worried about getting sunburned. Let's finish this quickly."

On the left: Medhi, wearing a pure-white bikini. She was putting her hair up, and getting ready to play some volleyball.

Their entrance drew cheers and stares. They stepped into the left court, glaring across the net at their opponents.

"Wait, it's just the two of you? Isn't there one more?"

"Mwa-ha-haaa! Wherever could the third one beeee? You'd better watch ouuut."

"Cower in fear of the enemy you don't see! Because even we don't know the third person's location!"

"Argh, don't explain thaaaat! Please, you've got to do something about that habiiiit!"

"So he's not here, then? Regardless, we mustn't let our guard down, but it sounds like we can focus on beating the two of you for the time being."

"Next question—what the heck were you guys thinking, challenging us to a beach volleyball match?"

"No reason not to tell you that. This was proposed by our coconspirator, Shiraaase!"

"This was Shiraaase's idea…? What?!"

"Ms. Shiraaase is cooperating with the enemy?!"

Both Wise and Medhi turned to glare at the referee's chair. Shiraaase returned a calm, sinister smile…

"Don't believe us? Well, it's true. Our primary goal is to send you packing. But…it's not that we're afraid of you or anything. We just would prefer to avoid armed combat. And this crafty lady picked up on that…"

"By which she means Amante ran her dumb big mouth agaaaain. And theeeeen, she suggested a beach volleyball maaatch."

"You mean… Oh, right. Well, without our weapons, we'd prefer to avoid combat, too, so this works for us…"

"It sounds like Ms. Shiraaase did a good job talking them into it."

The woman in the ref chair still had a calm, sinister smile, but… come to think of it, that was just her default expression. Nothing unusual here.

"So if we participate in this match, we get Porta's bag back. That's the deal, right? Is that true? Do you really have her bag?"

"We do. Sorella?"

"Right, riiiight."

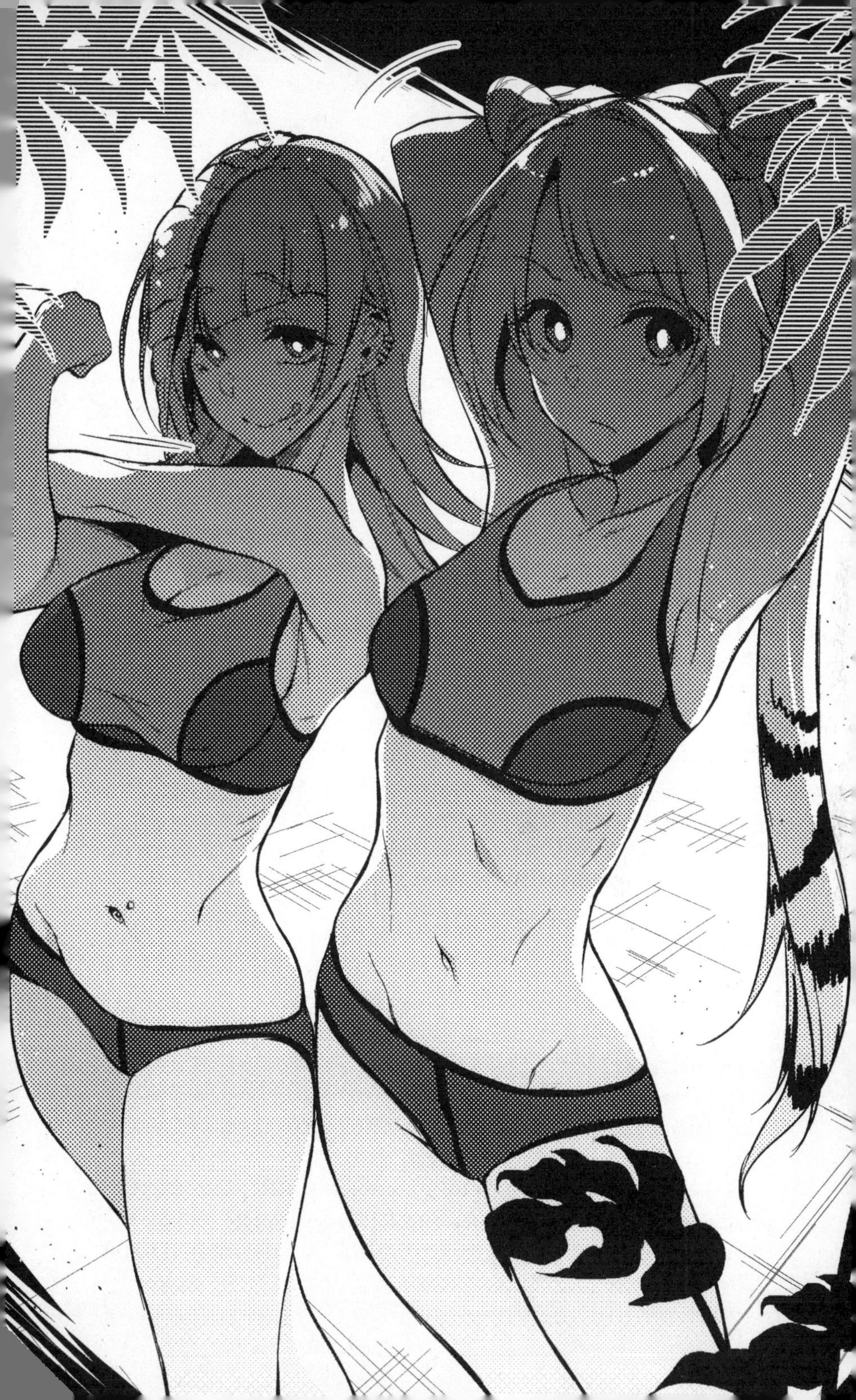

The magic tome hovering over the court tipped, and the bag came tumbling off.

It was a shoulder bag with a bunny doll hanging off of it. Amante caught it easily.

"That's really Porta's bag?"

"There's a chance it's a fake..."

"Sheesh, you people are suspicious of everything."

"Why don't you get it appraaaaised, then? Portaaaa! Come heeeere!"

"Huh? ...Oh, okay! I'll appraise it!"

Porta popped out of the stands wearing a frilly princess swimsuit and took the bag from Amante.

The second it was in her hands, she knew—no need to appraise it. A huge smile bloomed on her face.

"This is my bag! I'm sure of it!"

"The authenticity of the bag is proven! Okay, Porta, while we face off, you hold on to the bag."

"Don't lose iiiit! Don't even put it dooown!"

"Okay! I'll make sure to keep it safe! It'll never leave my side!"

She put the bag over her shoulders. Safe! Porta looked so happy she was practically hopping as she went back to the stands.

"Uh, I just had a thought...," said Wise. "Don't we now..."

"...have the bag back? Yes," answered Medhi.

"What are you whispering about? Let's get this match started!"

"If you wiiiiin, we'll give the bag baaack. But you don't stand a chaaance."

""Uh...sure..."""

Team Heavenly Kings vs Team Wise and Medhi!

The prize: the rights to the bag that was already back in Porta's hands!

Sorella made the first serve.

"Here goooes!"

As she jumped for the serve, the eyes of every man there snapped to her chest—she certainly wasn't lacking in that department, and the jiggle was more than noticeable. The ball, meanwhile, sailed safely over the net.

Wise was waiting for it.

"If it's the Libere Heavenly Kings we're fighting, that's reason enough! We're in this to win this!"

"Yes! Let's go!"

Wise with the bump. No accompanying jiggle. Medhi with the set. Quite a bit of jiggle. "Hah!" Wise with a powerful spike! Jiggle-free! However...

"Humph! Too easy!"

Amante moved too fast for the eye to see, stopping right under the ball.

She folded her arms and spread her legs, and the ball bounced up and away.

"Hey! That was... Oh, right! Your Reflection skill!"

"That's right! Any attack just bounces right off! With this skill and my superior physical abilities, the ball will never touch the ground! Now then...Sorella!"

"Right, riiight. Comiiiing. Aaand set!"

Amante jumped. Her incredible physical strength was about to deliver an incredibly powerful spike. Wise and Medhi braced themselves for a desperate save...

"Heh...just kidding." *Tap!*

""What?!""

She'd feigned a spike and then hit a soft lob. "She tricked us! Argh!" It sailed over Wise and Medhi's heads, dropping toward the back line. Wise lunged after it.

"Not happening! Rahhhh!"

She just barely made it. She had to do a headfirst slide in the sand to knock it up.

"Medhi, it's all you!"

"Got it! Hah!"

As the ball wafted upward above the line, Medhi went for the back row attack!

Arms built for melee damage sent the ball whistling just over the net. "Yiiiikes!" Right toward Sorella. Aiming for the weaker opponent! A spiteful blow.

But Amante was too fast. She was in front of Sorella in an instant, her reflection bouncing the ball away.

"I figured you would go for that, Cleric!" said Amante.

"Tch! She read me like a book!"

"Well, duh, you're notoriously evil! Of course you're gonna aim for the weak spot!"

"Shut up, Wise!"

"Thaaaanks, Amante! Riiiight! Seeet!"

"Take this! Hah!"

Amante jumped. This time she was definitely spiking!

"Medhi! Stop her!"

"Right! I swear I will this time!"

Wise and Medhi were breathing in sync up by the nets, desperately blocking—

"Just kidding." *Tap!*

Another soft lob sent the ball sailing mockingly over their heads.

"This again?!"

"You both suck! But we're not done yet!"

Wise desperately chased after the ball again, doing another headfirst sliding bump at the line! She'd made it in time once more!

And she knocked the ball over to the opponents' court.

Uh-oh.

"Perfect setup! You ready for this, Wise the Sage?!"

Amante's spike! The third time was true. A full-powered blow, so hard it nearly popped the ball, sending it flying at incredible speeds!

With no time to get up, Wise was still lying on her face! The ball bounced off her butt!

"Owwwwwwww!"

"Yes! Score!"

The ball bounced out of bounds. One point to Team Heavenly Kings.

Meanwhile, Wise and Medhi had lost a point. Wise's ass was done for.

There was a whole crowd watching, but she was waaaay past caring. She was rolling around, both hands clamped on her ass, wailing.

"Ahhhhhhh! M…my! My aaaaaahhh! My aaaaaaaassss!"

"Wise! Stand up! They scored a point, so they're keeping the serve!"

"Already doooone!" called Sorella.

"Wha?! Tch...I'm not letting you get a service ace!"

The ball was heading toward the line. Medhi went into a headfirst slide and barely managed to knock it up.

The ball went to the opponent's court. Amante was waiting for it.

"I'm not ending up like Wise! I've gotta get up and...eep!"

Medhi tried to scramble up, but she was unable to push herself off the ground.

All strength had left her body.

"Wh-why...? *Gasp!* Is this Amante's doing?!"

"I have noooo idea what you're talking abouuut! No Debuff skill heeere! Mwa-ha-haaa!"

"As if! You cheater!"

"Well, Amanteee? Finish them off for me, won't yooou?"

"Gotcha. Hah!"

Amante spiked! The ball crashed down like a meteor!

And slammed Medhi square in the butt! Critical hit!

"Ahhhhhhhhh! Aiiieeeee!"

"Bingooo! Amanteee! Nicely dooone! Aaaaah-ha-haaaa!"

"Heh-heh. Revenge is sweet. This is payback for you fooling around with our butts that one time!"

Clearly, she hadn't forgotten having her butt mistaken for a peach and savagely pawed at the day before.

But perhaps she should have considered the phrasing. Every man and woman in the crowd turned bright red as they looked from one team to the other. "I—I didn't mean it like *that!*" "She diiiiidn't!" The crowd wasn't that far off the mark, really...

But the match was still in progress.

"Keep it goiiiing! Make sure Wise never moves agaaain!"

"Wha—? Stop that! Augh, I can't even get up!"

"Sorella, summon some skeleton forces and make them bump it back."

"Got iiiit! If they return the baaaall, we can hit them over and over agaaain!"

Skeletal hands rose out of the court around Wise and Medhi.

Preparing for an execution.

"Make sure you go for Wise! Start with her!"

"Dammit, Medhi! Quit joking around!"

"Okay, you two! Kiss your butts good-bye!"

"Here goes my seeeerve!"

""Noooooooooooo!!""

Merciless focused attacks began raining down on the girls' backsides...

But then...

...Shiraaase blew her whistle.

"I'd like to infooorm you of a player change. Wise and Medhi are tagging out..."

A stir ran through the crowd. The new player appeared.

Luxuriously large, bountiful boobs. Firm backside covered by the base minimum amount of fabric.

Each step made the swimsuit ride up, and her fingers tugged it back.

All eyes snapped onto her. A roar went up from the crowd. Mamako took the court, outshining everyone there.

"Wise, Medhi, sorry it took me so long to change. But don't worry! I'll take it from here."

"M-Mamakooooo! Pleeeeease!"

"Please bring the hammer of justice! Be our ass avenger! Oh, but... you were so tired yesterday..."

"Thank you for worrying! But I'm fine now. I can do this! Go cool your behinds off! Porta, dear, could you help them out?"

"Yes! My bag's back, so I have all my items! Leave it to me!"

As Mamako stepped onto the court, the skeleton hands withdrew under the surface, almost like they were afraid of her. Porta came running out and pulled Wise and Medhi out of bounds.

By the side of the broadcast club seats, they managed to get to all fours, and Porta applied cooling gel sheets to their rear ends. "Eeeek!" "Ah-haah?!" They made weird noises, but that just proved it was working.

"My, what a relief! Now...I have some behinds to avenge!"

Mamako smiled at her opponents from the other side of the net.

Meanwhile, the sweat pouring down the Libere team's bodies

was unrelated to the workout they'd been getting. But they grinned through it.

"There you are, Mamako Oosuki! Let's make one thing clear: This is beach volleyball!"

"Not combaaaat! Follow the ruuules! And let's have fuuun!"

"Yes, I know. I'm here to play volleyball."

"So let me say one thing! We've got two! And you only have one!"

"Weee're children, and youuu're a mother, so two against one seems faaaair."

"Goodness, are we already ignoring the rules? Is that okay?"

Mamako looked to the ref's chair.

But Shiraaase never noticed. Her eyes were darting around the crowd, like she was looking for something...

And Sorella took that opportunity to serve.

"Here gooooes!"

The ball traced a gentle arc.

"How do I play volleyball alone? I can only touch it once...so..."

"She's gonna try to hit it back! My Reflection skill will cover it! Come at me!"

"Well, okay! ...*Hyah!*"

Mamako jumped near the net! A very mild spike. "Huh?" Such a warm, gentle spike that it caught Amante off guard and hit her in the forehead.

It barely bounced at all and just fell limply to the court at her feet.

"Uh, what??"

"Hee-hee! It worked. One point for me!"

"Amanteeee! What are you dooooooing?! You have to reflect it properlyyy!"

"Reflect... Oh, that explains it! My skill is *just* reflection!"

It only knocked things back as hard as they came in.

For a spike that gentle, the bounce back was equally weak.

"Well done, Mamako Oosuki! Still, that was a ridiculously weak spike..."

"Not at aaaall like Mamako. You can really tell her mom power's being restraaained. The special effect of our hideouuut. Seems like it's workiiiing?"

"And she burned too much power developing this island, so she's super worn-out. Heh-heh-heh. In that case—"

"I'm serving next, right? Here goes!"

Mamako's serve. "Okay! *Hyah!*" An easy arc over to the other court.

Meanwhile, Amante gave up on using her skill to reflect it, put her arms together, and bumped normally.

"Another wimpy hit! That clinches it! Mamako Oosuki can't use her usual strength at all! This is our chance!"

"Then let's do iiiit! Here goes, Amanteee! Seeet!"

"Find out what my full-strength attack can do!" *Poke.*

"Oh!"

The ball fell just inside the net. Mamako had been backing up, ready to receive, and she tried to dive forward. "Oops!" But—maybe because of exhaustion—her legs got caught in the sand, and she fell down.

She did manage to knock the ball higher, but it was a very soft lob, perfectly setting her opponents up.

"Crap! Mamako, get up!"

"She's aiming for you! Evade!"

"Mama! Run!"

The girls were screaming.

"...Hey, Mom?! ...Right, this is my chance...!"

A boy's voice came from somewhere in the distance.

Mamako's head snapped up, but she was still unable to get to her feet...

And Amante was leaping high into the air.

"I'm gonna make this moment count!"

"The Libere Rebellion will defeat this motherrr! This day will go down in historyyyy!"

"Mamako Oosuki's...butt! Prepare yourself! Hah!"

Amante's ass-destroyer spike exploded! The ball rocketed directly toward...!

"A mother's behind is no place for a ball!"

The sand next to Mamako suddenly moved, a cylinder rising out of it and batting the ball away.

The sand cylinder's shape evolved, branching, forming arms and legs—until it was humanoid, and then human.

The face perfectly mirrored Mamako's, but wore a slightly darker expression.

The size of her breasts, the curve of her figure, the firmness of her backside—all were identical to Mamako. The ultimate mom body sheathed in a swimsuit of the same design (just a palette swap.)

Hahako had appeared.

"...Huh?"

"Whaaaa?!"

"Oh my! Hahako! Perfect timing."

"It's been far too long, Mamako. I'm sorry it took me so long to get here; moving between servers proved quite a hassle. Can you still stand?"

"Yes, I'm fine. Now, then..."

The ball was falling toward her, so Mamako went for the set. Hahako followed with the attack.

Amante and Sorella were too stunned to move. The ball landed in their court. Point for Team Mamako and Hahako.

""Hee-hee! We did it!"" *High five!*

"Bleghhhh?! Hahako's heeeeere?!"

"Our mortal enemy! The one who keeps trying to make us her children! Shiraaase! Get Hahako out of here! Now!"

"This makes it two vs two. I was expecting this to happen, which is exactly why I contacted her in advance. Heh-heh."

"Bleghhhhh?! *Youuuu* summoned her here, Shiraaaaase?!"

"Why would you *do* that?! Aren't you on our side?!"

"I've betrayed you." Shiraaase didn't bat an eye.

"And without so much as a glimmer of guuuilt?!"

"Now, now, girls," said Hahako. "Parent-child volleyball will allow our hearts to communicate. I'll serve next!"

The match resumed. Hahako made a heartfelt serve.

A nice, gentle arc. A ball filled with a mother's love.

"Argh!" Amante said. "I can't receive *that*!"

She kicked it straight up.

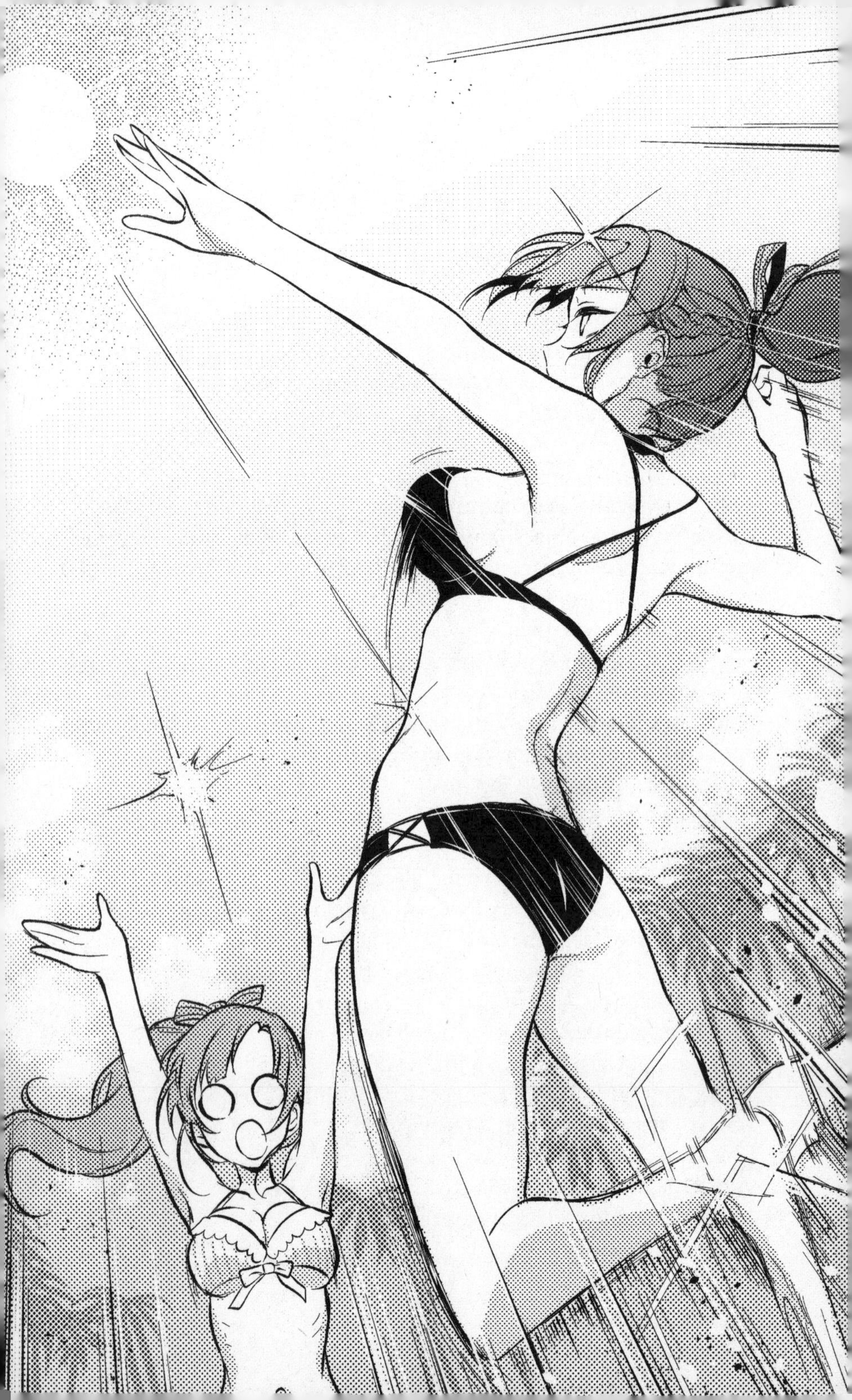

The ball rocketed skyward, even higher than the giant magic tome floating over the Libere side of the court.

"Hey, Amanteeee! What are you doiiiing?! I can't set thaaat!"

"No, Sorella. You're gonna give me the best set ever. We're way past being choosy about methods, got it?"

"What does that meeean? Ohhh…no, I get iiiit. Okaaaay."

Sorella grasped Amante's plan soon enough.

Just as the ball above was hidden behind the giant magic tome, Sorella quietly cast a spell.

"…*Spara la magia per mirare… Piombo Sfera!*"

And a ball fell from behind the magic tome…a suspiciously blackened ball.

Amante launched herself into the air, basically tackling the ball.

"Try and receive this, mothers!"

With a clearly metallic clang, the black ball was flung away, its trajectory changed.

It was now falling directly toward Mamako.

"Oh my! Receiving that seems like it would hurt a lot."

"Then let's change how we receive it. We'll play the same game they are! The rules no longer matter."

"Yes, it certainly seems like they don't. Porta, would you mind?"

"Okay! Mama, here!"

Porta came dashing over and handed Mamako a pair of Holy Swords. Hahako drew the same swords from the sand at her feet.

In the right hand, the Holy Sword of Earth, Terra di Madre. In the left, the Holy Sword of the Ocean, Altura.

Mamako and Hahako breathing as one. Each swung their Altura.

""One, two…receive!""

The power of water activated. Seawater pooled in front of them and then shot upward.

The black ball, knocked into the air by the geyser, hurtled toward the opponent's court.

"Waaaah! It came baaack!"

"I can reflect it! Sorella, get ready for the set! We're up against water…you know what that means?"

"I doooo! ...*Spara la magia per mirare... Calore Ardente!*"

The ball was reflected off Amante, and then Sorella's spell did the set.

The heat of the impact turned the ball red, and Amante used her reflection to attack!

"It'll vaporize water instantly! Good luck with—"

"Mamako, are you ready?"

"Yes! Here we go! One, two...receive!"

Mamako and Hahako swung their Terra di Madres together.

The sand on the beach gathered, forming a giant fist that punched the superheated ball back onto the other court.

"Dammit! Well, if that's how you wanna play..."

"We'll do iiit! We'll go all the waaay! Arghhhhh!"

The Libere team used the power of wind to attack!

"Ready, Hahako?"

"Yes. One, two...receive!"

To avoid the sand getting blown away, Mamako and Hahako hardened it with water, punching into the wind!

Such force! The rally wouldn't end!

Shiraaase was relaxing in the ref chair sipping tropical juice, but even she was getting slightly worked up inside.

"This is the most exciting beach volleyball match I've ever seen. Isn't it wonderful? Don't you agree, Wise? Medhi?"

"Uh...does this still count as beach volleyball?"

"It is still taking place on a beach, at least. So...maybe it half counts?"

"Mama! Hahako! Hang in there!"

The crowd was going wild. "Amazing!" "Keep it up!" "So many jiggles every—oof!" Some especially worked up men were being casually disposed of by smiling women, but the match itself was clearly a big success.

And finally, the moment arrived.

"I've had enough! Sorella! Full-power set...no, just slam it home and end this thing!"

"Okaaaay! ...*Spara la magia per mirare... Gruppo di Meteoriti!*"

The ball bounded off Amante's reflection, flying high into the air above, out of sight...

And then the atmosphere shook as meteor after meteor plummeted down.

"Everything falling is a ball! We're ending this right now!"

"If we're counting all of those as balls…that means…"

"We can ignore anything that isn't going to land in the court, and it'll count as Out."

"Er…waaaait?"

Anything that landed out of bounds counted as a point for Mamako and Hahako. "…Sorella." "Ooooopsie?" Sorella tried to cutely laugh her way out of it but it was too late to stop the meteor attack.

One, two, three, four. Meteor after meteor hit the water and the beach. "Retreat!" "Take cover!" "Whoaaa!" The first wave of meteors coffinized Shiraaase, and the girls quickly used her coffin for cover and scurried away.

Five, six, seven, eight. The beastkin crowd used their advanced physical abilities to scatter like baby spiders in all directions.

Nine, ten, eleven, twelve. A dozen meteor balls had already fallen out of bounds. Mamako and Hahako had scored twelve points in a row. With the previous points, their score was now fourteen.

"Match point. I do feel a little bad, but it's not good to spoil children when they're acting naughty, is it, Mamako?"

"I agree. And we have bottoms to avenge, so we must be strict here."

The hand of sand made with mom power lifted the two of them higher and higher.

The last meteor was falling directly toward their side of the court, and just before it passed them:

""One, two… Tut, tut!""

With hands on hips, and index fingers raised, the dual mom main cannons fired!

The light of a motherly scolding hit the meteor and changed the angle of descent, aiming it at the Libere court.

"I-i-it's coming right at uuuus?! Amante, pleeeease?!"

"Got it! My Reflection skill can… Uh, wait, I just remembered, that *Tut* didn't count as an attack, which means…"

Her Reflection skill wouldn't work on it.

"Ummm...theeen...good luck with iiiit, Amanteee! Byeeee!"

"Hey! Don't run away! Augh!"

As Sorella turned to run, Amante grabbed her, and they both fell face-first in the sand.

And the meteors landed right on their butts.

""N-noooooooooooooooooooooooooooooooooooo!""

Whoom. Direct hit. Kicking up massive quantities of sand and ocean spray all around.

Amante and Sorella were at the center of the crater, buried beneath the meteor...their fates unclear.

The moms had amassed fifteen points. The beach volleyball (?) match had ended in Mamako and Hahako's victory. The crowd (now at a considerable distance) let out a roar of celebration.

The two waved back...but then Mamako lost her balance. Hahako quickly caught her.

"Mamako, you're exhausted."

"You're right... It's so hard to use mom power on this island. Even with the swords in hand, the power just doesn't flow right... It's quite tiring."

"I couldn't sense a thing. But perhaps that just means I'm still not a real mom. What a pity. Either way, Mamako, you've got to rest. Don't strain yourself! You should replenish your Masato supply if you can."

"I'd love to... Let's try that. I swear I heard his voice a moment ago... I wonder where he went?"

Mamako turned to look and glimpsed a face in the crowd that quickly vanished out of sight.

"Whew, that was a close one... For her to pick me out of the crowd at that distance...Mom's son sensors are nuts."

He'd been at the very back of the crowd, where they'd retreated from the beach volleyball match. Dozens of yards away. Yet, she'd almost found him.

He had ducked down in time and, keeping his head low, backed into the jungle. With all this brush between them, she'd never spot him now.

"Looked like they already had Porta's bag back...so our problems are over."

Everything was resolved.

All without Masato's involvement.

"They could at least have said something to me before they got started... *Sniff*..."

No point dwelling on it. It wasn't like they had meant to leave him out. He hadn't kept his promise to his mother and hadn't been there when they got going. That was all there was to it.

Still.

"...Even if I had been there, I bet I wouldn't have had the chance to even do anything."

Masato *had* tried to push forward when Mamako had fallen over and was in real danger. But before he even took a single step, the crisis was averted.

All there was left for him to do was watch helplessly as Mamako battled her own fatigue, swinging the swords around, she and Hahako scoring an overwhelming victory.

There was literally nothing Masato could have done.

"Mom's actions solve everything. I just yell from the sidelines. That's how it always goes. I know! It never changes. So..."

He'd gotten used to it.

He tried to compartmentalize it like always, but it wasn't working. His head was spinning.

He'd felt frustrated with Mamako any number of times, but it felt different this time.

This irritation was directed inward.

"...This sucks."

The crowd was cheering for Mamako. The louder the cheers got, the worse Masato felt.

The fact that all he could do was watch was humiliating.

"I'm the hero chosen by the heavens! I'm not just anybody. In theory anyway."

He closed his eyes, and reached his hands to the sky, praying. Let the power of the hero of the heavens bring a great storm!

Then he looked up into the sky: It was blue, without a single cloud to be seen.

Irritatingly great weather. It was pissing him off.

"Yeah, yeah, I know! That's right. That's the truth. This is who I am. I can't do what Mom does. But…!"

Masato let out a long breath and broke into a run, turning his back on the beach and the crowds, heading deeper into the jungle.

He picked up a random stick as he went, moving faster and faster.

Roaring aloud, as if trying to convince himself.

"At this rate, things'll never change! I'm gonna be stuck to her forever! Even if we're apart, we're still family! The bond between us can never be severed, and a life spent in the shadow of the overwhelming force next to me will never end! Unless I do something!"

But what?

"I have to change! No matter what it takes, I have to obtain a power greater than Mom's! I have to change my world! And to do that…!"

He had to train. That was the only way. Instead of sulking, he needed to be patient and take things step-by-step. It was the only way forward that he could think of.

Masato swung, attacking the leaves in his way. "Rah!" His stick slammed home! He defeated the leaf!

"Yeah! The hero Masato leveled up! His sword skills leveled up, too!"

That's how it felt, anyway.

A tree branch was right in front of him, about to hit his face. "Not happening!" An attack that obvious would never hit him! He quickly twisted his body, avoiding the blow!

"Yeah! The hero Masato leveled up! His evasion went up a lot!"

In his mind, at least.

But feelings were important.

"All right, all right! I'm training! I'm getting stronger! Yeaaaah!"

Game objects contained no XP! All he was doing was trashing the jungle! But that didn't matter.

The feeling of wanting to get stronger was making this boy stronger!

Then.

"Mm? Something here… Oh, a monster!"

Thrashing through the brush, he'd stumbled across a man-sized horned frog. "Ribbit? Ribbiiiiiit!" It saw him, too. Its mouth opened, and its tongue snapped out like it was taking a quick, threatening jab at him.

Their battle began.

"It's much smaller than the last one... This one's weak...much like I am now... So I just have to beat you and aim for greater heights! Come at me, frog!"

"Ribbiiiiit!"

Stick vs tongue. Neither made an attempt to defend! They just rained blows upon each other.

Masato attacked! "Yah!" "Ribbit?!" **The horned frog took 1× damage! The horned frog attacked!** "Ribbit!" "Ow!" **Masato took 1× damage!**

Masato attacked! 1× damage! The horned frog attacked! 1× damage! Masato's attack: 1. Horned frog's attack: 1. Masato: 1. Horned frog: 1. Masato1 HornedF1 Masa1 Horn1 MaHoMahomaho...

Please wait for the battle to conclude.

But then...

"Guess I oughta step in here, sonny."

A cute, dazed-sounding voice. Tribal leather clothing. A small shadow running toward him.

No mistaking his kindred spirit anywhere.

"Fratello... Hey, wait, I don't need your help!"

"I ain't offerin' help. I'm stealin' your prey."

Yet, he stood shoulder to shoulder with Masato, ready for battle.

"You can't admit it, huh? Fine. Then let's say whoever finishes this thing off wins."

"You got it, sonny... Wait just one darn second. Something strange's goin' on..."

The horned frog moved. All four limbs planted firmly, it reared back.

"Ribbit ribbit! Croak croak! Crooooak!"

A call? Or a song? A moment later...

...a huge round thing fell from the sky over the jungle.

"What the...? Sonny, is that...?"

"Don't gawk, dodge! Argh!"

Masato grabbed Fratello and ran for it. He was really light. And smelled good. More importantly...

There was a thud that shook the earth. A truly giant horned frog had landed, much bigger than the one he'd been fighting. "RIBBIIIIT!"

"Mamaribbit!" The normal-sized horned frog hopped up on the giant one's head and looked down at it proudly.

"*Mamaribbit*? Did it call for its mom?"

"That there toad saw it was at a two-to-one disadvantage and went cryin' to mommy. Downright pathetic!"

"I'll say. Who calls in their mom? It's a child's mission to get stronger than their mother, no matter what it takes! You need to claim victory with your own hands!"

"Whoa... Ya sure got a way with words, sonny. That's exactly right. You're a real man. A manly man. Badass."

"Thanks, thanks. I'm a badass manly man."

Fratello's bleary eyes were wide open. There were sparkles in them. Masato grew bashful.

But this was no time to goof around.

"Now what...? Anything that big's gotta be strong. And have a lot more endurance than the one I was fighting... We might need a plan."

"Right, I'll attack! Mahhhhhh!" *Rumble*.

"Ah! Hey, stop that! If you use that move, I won't get to—"

Too late.

Fratello finished charging, ran forward, and struck!

"Mah!"

"Rib—?!"

His ultimate straight punch hit the mother frog in the gut...

...and, like an explosion, her bulk went flying. Knocking over trees in her wake, kicking up a swirl of leaves, heading toward the horizon—she was gone in the blink of an eye.

It left only a giant hole in the jungle and Masato on his knees.

"I still didn't get to do anything... Argh..."

"Early bird gets the worm. Don't blame me. So, sonny. I been thinking."

"...What?"

"I owe ya one, so…what say I teach you this power I got?"

His dazed eyes were staring up at Masato. He seemed a little excited.

"Ya said it yourself. *Get stronger than your mother, no matter what it takes.* That there sounded like your heart's deepest desire."

"Uh, yeah…that's right. That *is* my heart's deepest desire."

"Thought so. Truth is, that's exactly what my power's designed to do. So if ya want it, I'd be tickled to teach you."

"…You mean that?"

"I do. I've really taken a shine to ya, sonny. Your manliness, your goals, everything about you. So…"

Fratello suddenly threw a punch at Masato's face. "Whoa!" Masato caught the blow with his palm.

"I wanna fight ya once you're even stronger. That's my number one goal now, sonny!"

"And for the best possible face-off, you show your foe some humanity. You're a peculiar man, Fratello."

"I'm gonna take that as a compliment."

Masato didn't hesitate.

He yearned for power.

"All right. If you insist, I'd be glad to learn your power. But don't come crying to me if I end up even stronger than you."

"Humph. You sure got a mouth on ya, but that's what makes it fun. Let's get trainin'…"

But before Fratello could proceed…

"…Arghhh, once those two team uuuup, we can't wiiiin!"

"…Strategic retreat! Back to the lair to form a new plan!"

…there came what sounded like voices from far overhead. A square shadow passed over them.

"Uh, was that…?"

"They screwed up again? Good grief… Sorry, sonny. Urgent business just came up. I gotta go."

"Er…w-wait! I haven't learned your power yet!"

"I promise I'll teach ya tomorrow! Meet me here once the sun rises! That's a man-to-man promise!"

Fratello ran off through the hole he'd carved in the jungle. Then he turned back. "Promise!" he called, waving. Then he was gone.

"A man-to-man promise, huh? All right, then. I'll believe you."

Masato's new power had been postponed.

Night fell. The party was staying in the jungle cottage this time. But before bed…

…they'd dug a pit in the ground next to the building, shaping the tub with rocks and filling it with water.

In the center of this bath stood two Terra di Madres calling up the earth's heat.

In no time at all, they had a natural jungle hot spring.

And the heroes of the day were bathing in it.

"Well, as a mother myself, I certainly won't hesitate to accept the blessings provided by mom power."

Shiraaase had been the first to enter the water. Wearing a towel in the water was bad manners. She'd discarded hers immediately.

In the jungle night was the beautiful body of a working mother on full display. Round breasts like full moons. Slim, tight waist. Limbs as slick as vines. Shiraaase's body was beyond reproach.

Second in was Porta.

"Eep…I'm a little worried, but here goes! Hyah!"

With her bag firmly tied to her head, she splashed on in. "Eeeek! It stings!" Her arms and legs were a little sunburned after all that time in a swimsuit, so the heat of the water stung a little, but she got used to it soon enough and was smiling again.

But who would be the next to join them?

"I'd…like to take a bath, but…there's no way. It would kill me."

"I, too, will focus on staying cool. For the sake of my future."

Wise and Medhi elected to remain on the edge of the bath.

They had buckets of cold water and were soaking their behinds in them. These minibaths were a perfect fit for backsides still swollen from the ass-destroying spikes. "Fits a little *too* well…" "We *will* be able to get out afterward, right?" Like a glove.

Shiraaase gave them a sidelong glance, a faint smile on her lips.

"The battle was not without its casualties, but we did recover Porta's bag. I'm relieved."

"Thanks to your well-timed betrayal, everything went smoothly."

"To fool your enemies, fool your allies. And laugh about it later."

"You fool your allies by default, so this is hardly anything new."

"I sense a little spite in that reply! Thank you very much. Now, if you don't mind my talking to myself a bit here—this will be a monologue worth listening to."

"Don't let her trick you! Medhi, Porta, cover your ears!"

"If you listen, you'll end up getting mixed up in something!"

"O-okay! I'll be careful!"

The girls all placed their hands over their ears.

So Shiraaase just spoke louder, making sure they could hear her.

"MMMMMORPG (Working Title)...a game run with the goal of developing bonds between parent and child. There is an organization that stands against that goal, carrying out rebellious actions designed to plunge parent-child relationships into chaos—and even eliminate all mothers from the world."

"The Libere Rebellion, right? Wait, I can't hear you."

"Management has been conducting a series of investigations designed to uncover the scope of this organization and eliminate them once and for all. And at last, we've done it."

"Done what? Not that I can hear you, but be more specific."

Shiraaase nodded.

"I can proudly infooorm you that we've identified the mastermind behind all of these incidents. And we've located the hideout from whence the Four Heavenly Kings conduct their operations."

Everyone's eyes shot open and their hands left their ears.

This infooormation was far too important to let go unheard. They had to listen.

"The mastermind? Er, hang on...wait, wait. You know who gave my mom those weird powers?!"

"The one who sent my mother that weird staff that drove her crazy, messed me up, and nearly destroyed our relationship?! You know who they are?!"

"Th-that's incredible news! It's like you solved the case!"

"Yes, it is… We've figured it all out."

Shiraaase looked right at Porta, almost smiling.

But she quickly resumed her briefing. "We have all the pieces in place to take action. Management has created a plan to eliminate the Libere Rebellion and will soon set it in motion."

"You're already that far?!" cried Wise. "What's the plan?!"

"First, we destroy their lair. The reason I approached you this time is to ask for your help with that. After all, you're the experts in fighting the Heavenly Kings, and you possess inarguable battle prowess. Yes… what we need most is the cooperation of the hero Masato!"

Masato was the key!

"We need him! Our reliable leader, Masato!"

"Power so great he can even cleave the sky in two! Masato is absolutely necessary!"

"Masato is amazing! We really need Masato!"

"That's right. With Masato in the lead and all of you helping, we'll have you attack the Rebellion lair. And the target of that assault is on this very island."

"What, seriously? This island? They made their lair in *this* world?"

"We believe this was done to pull the wool over management's eyes. There are regular connection tests being done on all regional servers, whether they're ready for testing or not. It seems the Heavenly Kings have been using those to move around in secret. This is why we combed Catharn over without ever locating them. They got us good."

"But you've finally found them."

"There's some cunning trickery afoot, however, and the actual means of accessing the lair is still a mystery… That said, I've taken your accidental landing on this island as guidance from the heavens. And when you think of heaven…"

You think of the hero chosen by the heavens! Of course!

"The answer is obviously Masato!"

"Masato guided us here!"

"Masato's amazing!"

"He is! This is all thanks to Masato! Now that you have Porta's bag back and all your equipment, it's time for him to rise! Let Masato sound the call!"

"We must follow Masato!"

"All hail Masato!"

"I'm with Masato!"

His moment had arrived!

And yet...

"...He's *still* not taking the bait?"

Shiraaase sighed. Everyone looked in the same direction—Wise and Medhi both glaring, Porta with her eyes full of sparkles.

All four of them were staring at the shower area next to the baths.

"*Sigh*... Such bliss... I've never been so happy..."

He was seated resolutely on a bathhouse stool.

"Hee-hee! Well, do you have an itch anywhere? Tell me if you do!"

Unavoidable contact with large mom boobs pressing against his right arm as she shampooed his head.

"I had no idea washing a child's back was such a source of joy. This is a real education. Masato, if there's anywhere else you'd like me to wash, just say the word!"

And boobs every bit as large as his own mother's also unavoidably pressing against his left arm as she washed his back.

"*Sigh*... Man, this is the best..."

There was Masato, oblivious to the glares from all around, being thoroughly scrubbed by Mamako and Hahako at once. The one and only Masato.

"Hee-hee. What's gotten into you tonight, Ma-kun? You usually get so mad and yell at me to stop!"

"Oh well...part of me still feels that way, but... *Siiigh*... I'm just so blissed-out that I don't see the point in arguing..."

"I'm glad you're happy, Masato. Did something good happen?"

"Something did! Something totally did. Oh, right...Mom, Hahako, there's something I should tell you both."

""Oh? What is it?""

"I'm gonna go out early tomorrow morning. Not sure when I'll be back...but I should be back before evening anyway."

"You're going out? You mean... Oh, are you...?"

"Wait, wait, Mamako. I want to hone my motherly instincts. Let me say it."

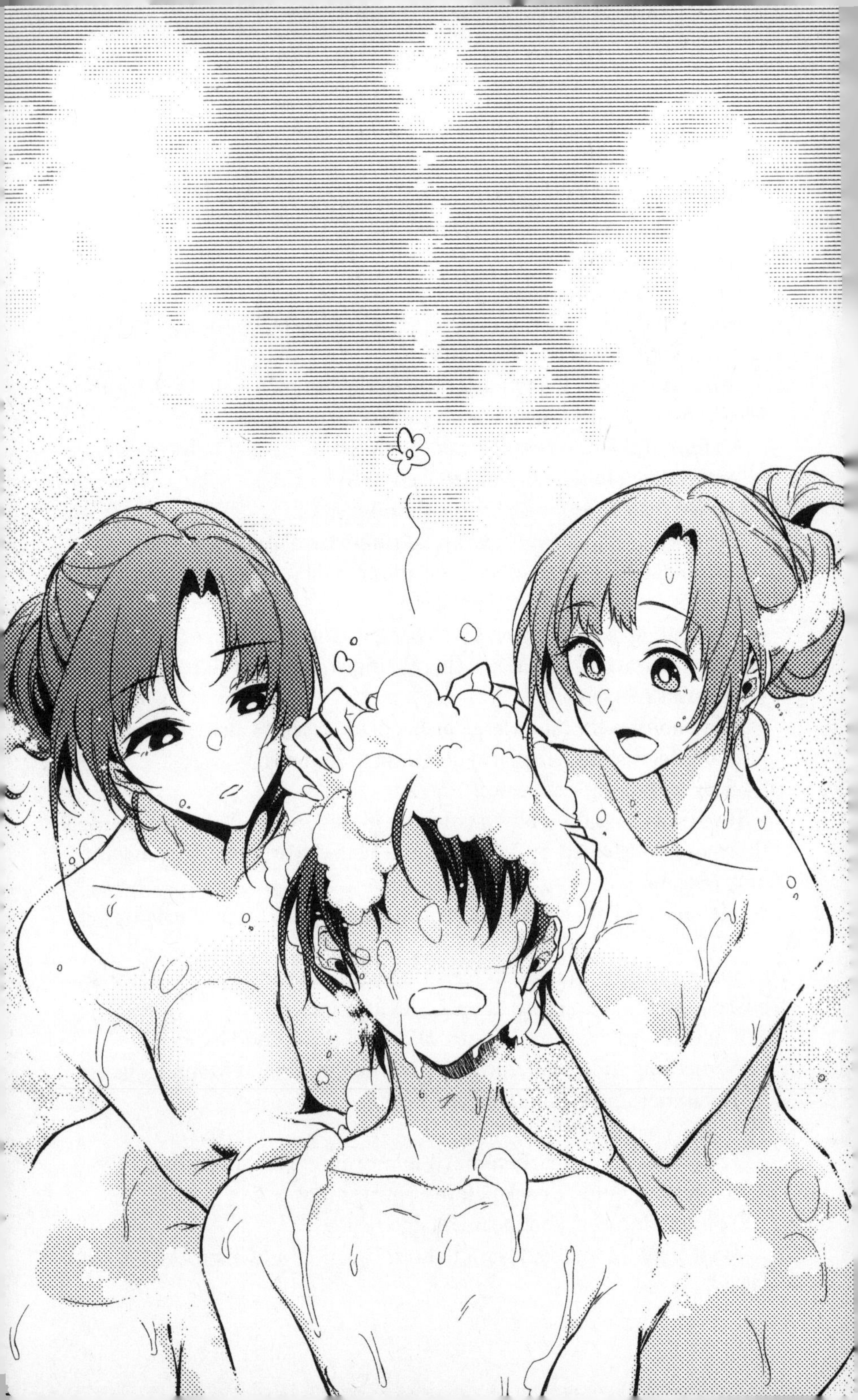

Hahako took a long look at the grin on Masato's face. Then it came to her.

"...I know! You've got a date."

"Uh, n-no... But, well...I am meeting someone, so..."

"Oh my! So that *is* a date! Ma-kun, won't you tell Mommy what this person's like?"

"Mamako, children don't like it if you ask that. My data indicates as much."

"Yeah, Mom. I definitely don't like that. It if all goes well, I'll be happy to show off later. Wait until then, okay?"

"R-right... Hmm... Still, I can't help but worry..."

"Mamako, at times like this, I believe all a mother has to do is make sure their child is clean as a whistle and send them out with a smile. My data says so."

"Hmm...yes, you're right. That's what I'll do."

They moved on from his head and back, washing his arms, legs, between Masato's legs—"Okay, cut that out!"—every bit of him.

Savoring the bliss, he stared up at the sky. *Oh, a shooting star.*

"Tomorrow...tomorrow I will obtain power...the power I've been longing for!"

He paid no attention to the three sets of baleful eyes boring into his very being.

Masato was on cloud nine as he waited for what tomorrow would bring him.

The Hero Masato Oosuki's Ultimate Move Development 3

Here's our Ten-Second Ultimate Move Development Corner! Today's instructor is Miss Porta! Thank you, Miss Porta!

R-right! I'll try my best!

PORTA

This time we'll be using your Item Creation skill to instantly create an ultimate move! Take it away, Miss Porta!

Okay! I don't know if I can, but if I imagine myself passing my skill to you... Nnggg...

PORTA

Can I use an ultimate move? I can use an ultimate move! An ultimate mooove...

Staaare...

WISE & MEDHI

Gasp?! Do I sense warm, supportive gazes?!

Chapter 4   I Pinched My Cheek. It Didn't Hurt. This Isn't a Dream! The Chronicle of This Son's Greatest Adventure Ever Begins!

It was so early, the sky betrayed only the slightest hints of dawn. Too early to even call morning.

But not to Masato.

"All right, morning! A bright, shining new day! Morrrrrrning!"

He bounded out of bed, washed his face, and polished off the breakfast he'd laid aside.

He finally had his equipment back, so he put that on and was ready to go.

"Well, Ma-kun. Anything you forgot? Your handkerchief? Or…"

"Got my weapons and armor! Everything I need!"

"Masato," said Hahako, "your collar's out of place. I'll fix it for you. Don't move."

"Thanks! …Right, now I'm ready!"

"Masato! I'm rooting for you! Good luck!" cheered Porta.

"Argh, it's not a date, okay? Ha-ha! Well, see you later!"

The moment he was out the front door he was shouting, "Yee-haw!" his engine at full speed as he made a beeline for the meeting spot. Mamako, Hahako, and Porta watched him go in their pajamas.

Looking so cheery that it seemed like he might start to literally glow, he plunged into the darkness of the jungle.

"Sheesh, he really went…"

"That he did… Oh, he tripped…and caught himself, laughing. Like everything in the world is a delight."

Wise and Medhi both looked half-asleep. They were pawing at their bedheads half-heartedly on the terrace, watching Masato go. Both sighed, thoroughly annoyed with him.

"I dunno if it's a date or not, but he's waaay too carried away."

"Heh-heh-heh. I can see you're curious. Maybe you should sneakily follow him?"

"Yeah, yeah, shove it, Medhi. That's not what this is. I'm just genuinely, purely, utterly disgusted. We're in the middle of a huge incident, but does that idiot care?"

"Clearly not," Shiraaase said, sounding quite vexed. "I'd very much like to convince him of the urgency of the situation."

She came striding out onto the terrace in a sexy black negligee.

"You're up, too... Wow, that's a racy getup."

"Sex appeal is the domain of a mature woman. It is important to regularly present yourself in a nearly nude fashion and observe the changes in your own body."

"So...this is a health thing? Never mind."

"Come to think of it, it's pretty rare for you to stay the night in this world, isn't it, Ms. Shiraaase?"

"Knowing we'd be launching an operation to the destroy the Rebellion lair, I left my daughter with my parents, allowing me to operate without regard to the hour. Yet..."

"Masato's being an idiot."

"His mind is elsewhere..."

"Yes. He's such a nuisance..."

All three sighed, shaking their heads.

Then...

"Masato's actions may not be entirely in vain," Hahako said, coming back into the room, Mamako and Porta behind her. "It may well be that he turns out to be invaluable to the execution of our plan."

"Hahako? What do you mean?" asked Wise.

"I mean exactly what I said. But I'd prefer not to share the details."

"You'd prefer... Why?" Medhi asked.

Hahako looked perplexed.

"My feelings on the matter are complicated, but...you're all getting ready to attack the Libere girls...and what they've done has certainly earned them that punishment. But to me, they're..."

"Your potential children," Mamako said.

Hahako nodded happily. "I have several pieces of information you're as yet unaware of. But if I were to share them with you, those girls would suffer. And the mother in me would prefer to avoid that. I may not yet be a mother, but I wish to honor my maternal instincts."

Hahako looked around the room and then bowed low.

Her children might be causing problems for others, yet they were still her children. She loved them all the same. To a mother, some things override conventional ethics.

"I think that's fine," Mamako said. "Any mother knows how that feels."

Smiling, she patted Hahako on the back, urging her to raise her head.

"You've mastered a mother's weaknesses, too. You're becoming even more like a mother, Hahako!"

"You think so? ...I'm so glad to hear you say that, Mamako."

"Shall we keep that spirit going?"

Mamako and Hahako smiled at each other, then, in unison, they cheered enthusiastically, ""Let's mom it!""—one mother and one mother-in-training.

"So, I hope everyone else is in. Wise, Medhi, Porta?"

"Uh...well...I dunno much about how moms feel..."

"While I'd prefer to be fully briefed, I don't want to force the issue."

"I think this is best! A mom's feelings are important!"

"Thank you. Ms. Shiraaase, what do you say?"

Shiraaase frowned, but...

"Disregarding my feelings as a mother myself...as management, I must throw up my hands. This game places the utmost importance on a mother's bonds, which makes it impossible for me to deny those feelings. This is information I would give anything to have, but even with it right in front of me, I clearly can't demand that you share it with us."

Shiraaase turned her back on Hahako. "But just in case, I'd better talk my superiors into the idea." She left the cottage, looking frustrated.

They bowed their heads after her.

"Well, I must be going," Hahako said. "As much as I enjoy your company, if I spend too much time with you, those girls will turn against me."

Hahako's feet melted into the ground. As a singular construct of the main system running the game, she was gone a moment later.

So.

"Well, what now? I certainly am worried about Ma-kun, but…"

"Yeah…I'm with you there. Not in a weird way—just…I have concerns."

"For all Hahako wished to avoid sharing information, she did tell us one thing."

"Yes! She said Masato's actions might actually be very important!"

"Right! Exactly! That's why I'm concerned!" Wise pounced.

"But Mamako's fussing is just her normal deal…"

"Especially since there's a chance Masato's on a date."

"Where could Ma-kun be? Where did he go? Who is he meeting? I just can't stop fretting about it!" Mamako began to fidget.

And when Mamako fidgeted, the ground beneath her feet quaked…

"Stop!" "Mamako, calm down!" They managed to stop Mother Earth from answering her call.

"Whew… We need you to keep your head, Mamako."

"I know! Let's borrow the power of the earth and find out where Ma-kun is! Porta, could you get me my swords from your bag?"

"Okay! ……Um, let's see here……" *Rummage, rummage.*

"She didn't calm down at all! Don't! You can't use A Mother's Fangs!"

"You'll find out where Masato is, but totally mess up whatever's going on there!"

"So instead, let's try *that* approach…right, Medhi?"

"Yes. This time…we need to be stealthy."

Judging from their smiles, both girls loved that sort of thing.

In the pitch-black jungle, guided by the hand of fate, Masato reached the promised spot!

Or at least, he wanted to claim as much, but actually he'd just sort of run around until he stumbled across it. He'd headed in the general direction until he found the damage their combat had incurred.

Masato stood staring at the giant jungle hole Fratello's attack had created.

"That's no ordinary power... The force is simply incredible. And my kindred spirit is going to teach me this move? Where is he?"

He found a place to sit down, and it felt like he'd been waiting around two hours or so, but there was still no sign of Fratello. This was entirely Masato's fault for showing up way too early.

Through the gaps in the broccoli above, he could see blue skies. Morning had definitely broken.

Any minute now...

"Sonny! You're already here?"

"Oh, Fratello! I've been waiting!"

Fratello appeared farther down the giant hole, walking toward him.

He gave Masato a long look with those dazed eyes of his and nodded approvingly.

"Mornin', sonny. I see you kept our man-to-man promise."

"I mean, I am a man, after all. I keep my word."

"Mm. Still, ya sure dressed for the occasion."

"Heh-heh, well? This is my true form."

Long jacket. Gauntlet on one arm. The Holy Sword of the Heavens, Firmamento, at his hip.

Fully equipped, Masato struck a proud pose! *Shiiiing!*

Fratello looked at Masato and then down at his own leather garb and sighed.

"You ain't too hot in that, sonny?"

"Honestly, yeah, I'm burning up under all this. I was thinking about taking it off...but this is my equipment! I can't just ditch it!"

Even just sitting still in this had worked up quite a sweat.

"Well, in that case, we'd better relocate."

"Relocate? We aren't training here?"

"If we train here with you dressed like that, you'll die of heatstroke. I know a place that's a mite cooler. Come check out my lair."

"Uh...your lair?"

"I'll put my own equipment on. I've got some really badass gear, specially made for me. Let me show it off for ya!"

Not a house, hotel, or inn, but a lair.

That bugged Masato a bit, but... "You comin' or not?" "Oh, wait up!" Fratello was already moving, so Masato followed close behind.

*   *   *

A while later…

Porta poked her head out of the brush near where Masato and Fratello had been.

With her keen eyes, she looked around, first to the right, then to the left, then to the right again.

"Hnggg… I think it's safe to step out!"

Back in her usual garb, the shoulder bag secured to her back, Porta jumped out of the brush.

After her came Wise in a crimson jacket; Medhi in a white healer tunic; Mamako with a few pieces of armor over her favorite dress; and Shiraaase in her usual nun habit.

All of them were drenched in sweat.

"It's so hot! I feel like all the moisture is being wrung out of me."

"Perhaps putting all our gear on in case of trouble was a mistake. Wise, can you cool us down?"

"No prob. *Spara la magia per mirare… Vento Fresco…*"

She sounded exhausted, but the spell activated. It wasn't the strongest effect she'd ever managed, but a cool breeze blew past them.

A look of relief spread across their fatigued faces.

"Oh, that's nice! It's so helpful having you around, Wise."

"You're a huge help! Thank you, Wise!"

"Even I have to admit it this time. I'm genuinely glad we have you, Wise."

"Wow, even Medhi? …Man, you're making me blush…"

"No need to be embarrassed! You're a human air conditioner."

"Dammit, Shiraaase! You just ruined it."

"You so rarely get to use magic in combat… Perhaps you should change your job to 'Air Conditioner Technician.'"

"I'm not changing jobs! And that's hardly our focus here…"

Wise pointed at the giant hole in the jungle.

"…That kid with Masato. Same one, right?"

Mamako, Porta, and Medhi all nodded.

"Yes, I'm sure of it."

"I agree!"

"Sorry, I'm lost…"

"Oh, right, Ms. Shiraaase, you weren't there. Let me expl—I mean, infooorm."

"Medhi, is that a challenge?" asked Shiraaase. "Are you aiming to steal my role from me?"

"I'm just following your lead! Anyway, please listen. When we were developing the resort, we stumbled across two of the Heavenly Kings…"

And a sudden intruder had blown Mamako away one-handed.

And that intruder…

"Fratello… Come to think of it, the other two Heavenly Kings dropped that name. Supportive evidence."

"That clinches it… This Fratello's the third of the Four Heavenly Kings," said Wise.

"When we encountered him, he spoke very differently…but I suppose we should assume this is a plot to entice Masato to their side."

"Just like a certain someone we know who tried to honey trap Masato. So evil."

"Those were my mother's orders, and not my choice." Medhi's smile twitched.

"Ow, ow, ow, stop it, you evil beauty! Your staff is grinding against my foot!"

"Hmm…I'm not so sure… It didn't seem like he was faking it…"

"I thought they seemed like real friends, too!"

"I had the same impression but let us put such doubts aside for now. We have more pressing matters to attend to."

Shiraaase began walking.

"They said they were headed for Fratello's lair. This is our opportunity."

"True! If the enemy's gonna lead us there himself, we can't let that go to waste."

"And if this leads to our discovering how they get around, that would be perfect."

"Exactly. Come on!"

All fell silent, tailing Masato and Fratello as quietly as possible.

*   *   *

Meanwhile, those being tailed…

"Signs of suspicious activity nearby are…all clear."

"Can't say the same for you, sonny, but no one slips by a man like myself unnoticed."

"Don't underestimate my detection skills. They're even better than yours!"

"Fat chance—mine are the best."

Shoving their shoulders into each other, each stubbornly insisting he was better, the two boys pressed onward.

The jungle gave way to a rocky area filled with boulders and potatoes.

The road grew steep and the terrain uneven, but it was definitely a doable climb. Skirting the edges of the giant boulders and potatoes, they made steady progress.

In time, they reached a sheer rock face.

"Looks like a good spot for rock climbing… Where to next?"

"Ain't no next. This here's the entrance to my lair."

Fratello put his hand on the sheer rock face.

A moment later, a hole just wide enough for a person to pass opened up.

"Um…wow, how's that work?"

"Nothin' special. Just a touch. Works for those of us living here and any undead monsters in our employ."

"Uh…why undead monsters?"

"One of my folks is good at controlling undead monsters, so we made the door work for 'em. Course, if ya ask me, they're too wimpy to do us a lick of good."

"Weird skill to have… Hmm…"

A flicker of doubt passed through Masato's mind.

"C'mon, sonny! It's a real maze inside. You're gonna get lost if you lose sight of me."

"R-right…"

Masato wiped the sweat from his brow—caused not by heat, but by the turbulent emotions he was experiencing. Then he followed Fratello into the lair.

*　　*　　*

The cave interior was a gentle downslope. There were magic stones placed here and there, glowing softly.

A zombie hoard appeared before them, but when they saw Fratello, they shuffled aside.

The road beyond split in two, and the path they took split in three, and again beyond that.

"...This really is a maze."

"Even we get lost sometimes! This one dope got turned around and ended up running all over this here cave. Didn't get back till she'd gotten up close and personal with every single cave. But she's got some wicked fast legs, so it only takes her a few minutes to run places."

"So...really high physical attributes...but really dumb..."

"Come to think of it, that same dolt said somethin' about getting fed up with it all. She set about making somethin'... I feel like I saw it placed right by the entrance... Did ya see it, sonny?"

"No, I didn't see anything. I was kinda preoccupied..."

The cool breeze on his cheeks had gone from comfortable to downright chilly.

After several more branches, the rock and dirt floor gave way to carefully laid tiles. The ornately decorated walls and ceiling had clearly been crafted by skilled artisans...

Fratello had Masato had reached the entrance to some sort of church, all lit up by colorful magic stones.

"Like an underground shrine..."

"Not much of a shrine, since ain't nothin' here being worshipped... Though I guess there is somethin' special resting here. One heck of a treasure."

"Treasure?"

"Interested, sonny? Rightfully so. You go through a cave, see a room like this, hear there's a treasure, any man would get excited."

"Yeah, well...that's part of it..."

"Okay, then. I'll let ya have a peek. This way, sonny."

Fratello walked off, humming. He told some patrolling skeleton knights to keep up the good work.

Masato followed at a safe distance.

Crap. I'm in real trouble here.

Deep down, he was already sure.

He was sure, but he didn't know *how.*

Where had he gone wrong? Half his brain was going back over events, trying to figure it out.

But the rest of his brain was desperately trying to think of an escape plan.

The two trains of thought were tripping each other up, making his head spin.

"Here we are! The treasure!"

Masato's legs had carried him there without him noticing. A massive door stood open before him.

His eyes focused on a dark glimmer.

"Wha... Th-that's..."

It was some sort of laboratory—science? Sorcery?

And a pretty big one, at that. There was a giant magic circle on the floor with cords of all colors tracing its lines, which led to a number of pedestals arranged around the magic circle.

And in the center of the circle was a gelatin sphere over ten yards in diameter.

"Mwa-ha! Your eyes are poppin' right outta their sockets, sonny! Ya look like ya just seen a ghost."

"Uh, yeah... This is a surprise, I mean... Holy crap..."

"Go on in. Relax a spell. I'm just gonna change real quick."

Fratello dashed off.

Masato stepped into the room, looking at the nearest pedestal.

There was a dark gem on it the size of his fist.

"That gem's...definitely the one Amante and Sorella used."

It was one of the unofficial items that could control any NPC, overwriting their behaviors or turning them into monsters. They had been used against them any number of times.

There was a **Now Loading** message displayed on the pedestal. The dark gem seemed to be downloading something.

There were cords running from the pedestal beneath the gem to the magic circle. He followed them carefully, moving closer to the source—that giant sphere. He stared into the sphere's depths.

Lines of computer code were swimming around inside like sea snakes.

"The dark gem is downloading this data... A program? I have no idea what that means, but if this program lets them control NPCs... Wait, I thought..."

When they'd first gone up against Sorella at her casino, they'd been hired to recover a program that controlled character settings. It was one that had been stolen from management.

This Alzare document had been successfully recovered, thanks to Masato's own heroics, but...

"Was it actually a fake? No, no, no, no! It couldn't have been! Shiraaase verified it! So they secretly made a copy! That must be it! Yeah. I couldn't have screwed that up! I didn't!"

His voice rose into a shriek that echoed through the room.

He felt much better afterward. Calm.

"So this is where they manufacture the dark gems. And the lair itself..."

...was the Libere Rebellion's hideout. Sad, but clearly true.

And Fratello...

"Damn. What now? What should I do?"

Masato stared blankly around the room.

Nothing came to mind.

Meanwhile, outside the lair entrance (which was disguised as a totally ordinary wall):

"Here goes! ...*Spara la magia per mirare... Alto Bomba Sfera!*"

Wise's spell unleashed a massive amount of energy.

It scored a direct hit on the rock face, causing a tremendous explosion. The backwind rushed past them, blowing all nearby boulders away.

"Ow!" One of the boulders hit Wise in the forehead. **5 damage!** Moving right along...

The wind blew the dust away, leaving behind a pit where the explosion had occurred.

But the rock face itself was unharmed. There weren't even any scorch marks.

"Tch! Now I'm really pissed."

"Wise, let me try next."

Medhi emerged from behind a giant potato. Player Change! Medhi stepped up to the rock face, smiling broadly, like the beautiful girl she was.

THUD, THUD, THUD, THUD. A series of yakuza kicks! "Ow!" The winds stirred up by the kicks sent another boulder into Wise's head. **9 damage!**

The beautiful girl's strikes seemingly had more force behind it than the spell did, so maybe... But no.

The rock wall was unharmed. Not so much as a footprint was left behind.

"Even my power can't damage it... How frustrating."

"If it actually had, I probably would've died from the shock... Either way, we clearly aren't smashing our way through. *Sigh*... So annoyinggg..."

Wise waved to a nearby giant potato.

Mamako and Shiraaase came out from behind it, joining them.

"Good work, both of you! As a reward, I'll rub both your heads!"

"Yaaay! Thanks! ...I mean, I always like head rubs, but we failed, so..."

"Masato and Fratello definitely went in from here. This is clearly the entrance. But..."

"...The path won't open without the conditions being met. This is a problem...coming all this way only to get stuck here... How vexing."

Shiraaase hung her head. Her disappointment was contagious. The other three hung their heads, as well.

Next to them...

"I wonder if there's a special effect on it! Even my eyes couldn't appraise it. I'm gonna take another look!"

Porta went alone toward the rock face. "Hnggg..." She gave it a long stare. A looooong stare. She scanned every inch of the rock face, determined to find something.

But she couldn't find anything. So sad.

"Awww… I wasn't useful at all…"

Dejected, Porta put her hand on the rock and hung her head. "Fwah…" She sighed.

Then…part of the rock in front of her vanished, and a hole appeared.

"Huh? …Whoa! It opened! It opeeeened!"

"Wait, for real?" said Wise. "Wow, it actually did! Porta, nice work!"

"Oh my! That's amazing, Porta! How'd you do it?"

"Um…I just touched it! And it opened!"

"Just by touching it? That's…like… Um…" Medhi trailed off.

Shiraaase put a hand on her shoulder and quietly shook her head.

"Never mind that! Our path is open! Let's hurry in. Come on! Let's go! Yahoo!"

"Ms. Shiraaase…you're being a little too obvious. Do you know something?"

"Yes. I do, but I had carelessly forgotten. There was a simple solution all along, but I was too busy panicking to think of it. I have much to learn."

"I would love to hear more about this."

"I must ask for your patience. The contents are quite shocking…and I'm at a loss regarding how best to share them."

Shiraaase looked over at Porta. "That tickles!" squeaked Porta. She was getting dual squeezes from Mamako and Wise and looked to be having the time of her life.

Medhi glanced at Porta, and a shadow passed over her face.

"Very well," she said with a sigh. "I'll defer to your judgment on this."

"Thank you. In appreciation for keeping this on the down-low, I may ask for your assistance later. Heh-heh-heh."

"I-if you mean what I think you mean, that may be quite a challenge…"

"Intelligence carries its own trials. I do appreciate it. That said… Mamako, Wise, Porta! We should get moving. I'm concerned about Masato."

"Oh, yes! I'm so worried about Ma-kun!"

"I'm less worried about Masato than what'll happen if Mamako gets too worried about him. Let's infiltrate this enemy lair!"

"Yes! Let's go!"

Porta had the sharpest eyes, so she took the lead. The party filed into the dimly lit cave.

Weapons in hand, caution at the max.

"Careful, everyone... This is the Rebellion hideout...," Wise warned. "Who knows what sort of traps they have lying in wait."

"That's right...," agreed Medhi. "And it's so dark here... I wouldn't be surprised if there are undead monsters roaming about."

"Hmm...about that. I've been thinking..."

"Mm? What is it, Mamako?"

"This is where Amante and Sorella live, right? If they have traps and monsters everywhere, wouldn't that be terribly inconvenient? If they had some helpful means of getting to the center of this lair quickly, then it might make more sense, but..."

Mamako tilted her head, looking confused.

The rest of the party stopped, thinking this through.

"No way," Wise said, shaking her head. "Not that I don't get your point, Mamako. I mean, sure, you wouldn't want to prep traps and monsters and put them in your own way. That would be dumb. But... that's how RPGs work."

"Everyone who enjoys these games realizes this at some point and simply accepts it as a tacit understanding," said Shiraaase.

"Even in one's own domain, it's basically common practice to never have a convenient transport device," added Medhi. "There's no chance of there being one here."

"Nope."

"Never."

"Absolutely not."

"Oh! I found one!"

"""Whaaaat?!"""

Porta was pointing at a spot a few yards inside.

There was a wooden sign on the wall that read: NOT THAT I NEED TO EXPLAIN THIS, BUT THE TRANSFER CIRCLE IS THIS WAY! It also had a giant arrow pointing down the passage.

When they followed it, they found themselves in a small room with a magic circle on the floor.

Mamako's party found a convenient transport device!

"Yes, I knew it! This is ever so helpful. Hee-hee."

"But why…? Oh, right…"

"This is the lair of the Four Heavenly Kings."

"The hideout of a bunch of idiots."

"It goes directly to their living quarters! I can operate it!"

Mamako and Porta both beamed. Everyone else looked tired already. All of them stepped into the circle.

"It's voice operated, so I'll do it! Ready? *Initiate Transfer!*"

At Porta's call, light enveloped them.

A moment later, the transfer was complete.

"Whew, that was easy… So, where are we?"

"Oh my! This place is lovely!"

They were in the middle of an elaborately decorated passage, like a palace or shrine. There were elegant magic stone lamps all around them, evenly spaced and providing plenty of light.

There were four doors in the passage—two on each side.

The doors on the right were labeled I and II.

The doors on the left were labeled MAN and IV.

"This is the common area, and these are the Four Heavenly Kings' rooms?" said Wise.

"That seems fair…but why is one of them labeled *Man*?" asked Medhi. "That's just…baffling."

"Whatever. Let's take a quick look around. Carefully… We don't want to just bump into an enemy here."

No sooner had the words left Wise's mouth than the door marked MAN swung open.

"What's all the ruckus? Y'all… Ahem, you must be very foolish to make such a racket outside my room."

Halfway through his speech, he corrected his manner of speaking. He went from cute to cold in an instant.

Fratello was in Libere Heavenly King mode, wearing an oversize black coat, both sleeves and hem much too big for him.

"……Mm?" And he ran right into Mamako's party. Both sides looked surprised.

Gasps all around.

"Oh, where are my manners? Hello, Fratello. So sorry to intrude."

"Oh, right, hello." Fratello reflexively responded. So proper! "No, wait…why are you here?! How did this happen?!"

"Crap, we already bumped into someone!"

"And this one…the worst one. Ms. Shiraaase, Porta, you'd better get back."

"Splendid idea. Porta, let's go."

"R-right! Don't want to interfere with the fight!"

Shiraaase and Porta tried to hide in one of the opposite rooms. But this was the worst choice.

"Hey, Fratello! What are you yelling about? Keep it down!"

"We're busyyyy! It takes a lot to heal after getting hit by a meteooooor! We need peace and quiiiiet!"

The doors opened. Amante emerged from I and Sorella from II. Both Heavenly Kings had cooling gel sheets plastered all over them.

"Owww… It still stings… Wait, what?! You're—"

"Wh-wh-why is Mamako heeeeere?! Whyyyy?!"

"How bad is this gonna get?!"

"Three of the Four Heavenly Kings, all at once!"

"Oh my! Amante, Sorella, don't strain yourselves. Rest as much as you like!"

"No, no, Mamako, don't be nice to the enemies!"

"You mean it? I could really use the rest."

"Honestlyyyyy? It hurts to even moooove."

Amante and Sorella went back into their rooms.

"Um…they're actually listening?" said Medhi. "Well, as you were, then."

"W-we were joking! We're not falling for such an obvious trick!"

"R-riiiight! We didn't fall for iiit!"

They clearly had, but they hastily turned back. ""Owwwww!"" They were swiftly removing the cooling gel sheets, trying to look like Heavenly Kings again.

Fratello, Amante, Sorella, all three together, braced for any sudden movements.

"Mm? Where'd Porta and Ms. Shiraaase go?"

"Seems they snuck into room IV."

"They didn't come rocketing back out, so I guess that room was safe?"

"Oh, good. Well, first, where is Ma-kun?"

"They're not gonna answer just because you ask."

"Then we'll just have to force them to!"

Wise pulled out her magic tome. Medhi raised her staff. Ready for combat!

"Um…let's talk first…" Mamako pushed for diplomacy, but they cut her off, stepping forward.

However, none of the Heavenly Kings went for their weapons. They looked totally calm.

"Never thought you'd manage to get into our lair… What a blunder. But in a sense, it works in our favor. This place is filled with secrets all designed to defeat Mamako Oosuki."

"Fratello's right! This our hideout! The master designed the place to make it next to impossible for you to use your motherly powers! Here, you're a shadow of your usual self! And if we use our trump card… Heh-heh-heh…"

"Alsooooo, it's based on my Debuff skiiiill. All thanks to meee. That part's important, so take noooote."

"Both of you, shut up. Stop explaining things! …Let's do this. Time for a taste of hell!"

"Oh my! This does sound bad. Wise, Medhi! Be careful!"

They braced themselves. The Heavenly Kings surrounded them.

They all wore malicious grins as if their victory was assured.

Amante moved first, holding out a hand and chanting.

"She who rejects mothers, Anti-Mom Amante, wills it so!"

Then Sorella joined her.

"She who scorns mothers, Scorn-Mom Sorella, wills it soooo!"

Finally Fratello.

"He who threatens mothers, Frighten-Mom Fratello, wills it so!"

In answer to their call, a magic circle appeared at the party's feet. The pattern looked suspiciously familiar…

The Libere Heavenly Kings all put their hands on the rim of the circle, and, as one…

""""Initiate Transfer!""""
They activated the transport spell.

"Wait, this isn't some secret art?!"

"It's just a transport spell?!"

"Oh my... Where are they sending us? Oh, maybe to where Ma-kun is!"

"You're waaay too optimistic, Mamako! Oh crap!"

A burst of light surrounded the three of them...

Meanwhile, in room IV.

Shiraaase and Porta had their ears to the door, listening.

"...I can't hear anything."

"There's no way to tell what's happening outside!"

"I'm concerned...but it would never do to show ourselves and get in the way of the fight. We'd better wait quietly in here until Mamako infooorms us that it's safe to come out."

Shiraaase looked around the room.

It was fairly large, with a bed, shelves, couch, and table—all quite fancy looking.

Based on all the stuffed animals, this was a child's room.

"...Ah!"

Porta yelped and ran over to the couch. She picked up the giant teddy bear lying there, hugging it while her eyes sparkled.

"You like that one?"

"I've wanted this stuffed animal for ages! Ever since I started playing the game! But I could never figure out how to get it...!"

"Hmm, I see... This room is filled with things that would delight you... Is that a coincidence, or...?"

"Oh! S-sorry! This is no time for playing with toys!"

"No, go ahead. It's given me the glimmer of an idea."

The idea was almost more of a wish.

Shiraaase moved over to Porta.

"Is the leader of the Libere Rebellion available?" she asked. "I'd like to talk."

Porta turned around, looking surprised. Shiraaase pretended not to notice.

"Management is aware of your true nature. Our evidence..." She began tickling Porta.

"Eeeek?! Aughhhh!"

"This will lead us to the truth." Her assault continued.

"M-Ms. Shiraaaseeee?! That reeeally tickles!!"

Shiraaase's fingers danced over Porta's cheeks and neck as the girl squirmed. But still the tickling continued.

Until...

"...Cease this foolishness. State your business."

A whirl of darkness had appeared in front of Shiraaase. The voice that emerged was unearthly, androgynous.

"Eep?! Wh-what's that?!"

"You were monitoring her, then? I thought so."

"I said...state your business."

"Then let me be brief. We're in the midst of an operation to eliminate the Libere Rebellion. Our investigators will reach you momentarily. Before that happens, I have a proposal."

"...Namely?"

"If we say the incidents you caused were necessary to restore parent-child bonds, wouldn't that resolve everything tidily?""

".........!"

The sound from within the swirl sounded like a gasp.

The proposal had certainly gotten a reaction. Shiraaase pressed the point.

"If that's the reason for it, then myself and management will not hesitate to cooperate. Please consider it."

"That's not—"

"It *is* possible. There is precedence, as you're well aware. Given the scale of the incident, the penalty will be significant...but if we place parent-child bonds first..."

"If that were possible, I'd never have had to do this in the first place!"

The voice was suddenly a shriek.

Overwhelmed, Shiraaase fell silent.

"...Shirase, take that girl and evacuate the island at once. Please."

This was almost a whisper. The swirling darkness vanished.

Diplomacy had failed.

Shiraaase stood stunned for a moment and then let out a disappointed sigh.

"...It appears I stepped in something I shouldn't have. Quite a blunder."

"U-um, Ms. Shiraaase?" Porta looked up at her, really confused. Her eyes spoke volumes. Anxious eyes, staring up at her, pleading for an explanation.

But Shiraaase pretended not to notice. Again.

"Work talk. Don't worry about it." *Tickle.*

"B-but! I-I-waaahhh! That tickles!"

"Pay it no mind." *Tickle, tickle.*

"B-but...eeeek!"

"Pay it no mind." *Tickle, tickle, tickle, tickle, tickle.*

"O-okay! I won't! I won't, so stopppp!"

This was not silencing her by force. This was a reward for being a good girl! "A little extra." "Eeeeeeek!" Porta was all smiles. It was a reward for sure!

Now, that's enough of grown-up duplicity.

"At any rate, my business is concluded. The rest lies in Mamako's hands..."

Shiraaase put her ear to the door, searching for sounds outside. She couldn't hear any signs of battle. The entire time they'd been hiding in the room, there'd been no sounds from the hall.

"What on earth is going on out there...? Perhaps just a peek... Oh?"

She opened the door and peered through the crack...

...and found no one outside.

The Hero Masato Oosuki's Ultimate Move Development 4

Sigh... The World Matriarchal Arts Tournament was the only time I've managed to use that hawk attack... Is acquiring an ultimate move really too much to ask...?

SHIRAAASE

Not at all.

HAHAKO

Masato, hold your head high.

Shiraaase! And Hahako, too!

SHIRAAASE

Acquiring an ultimate move is possible... If you swear loyalty to me and promise to do whatever I say, I will secretly arrange for it. Heh-heh-heh.

HAHAKO

You just have to become a being created by the main system, like I am. Then you can use ultimate moves whenever you wish.

Sign a contract with the devil or abandon my humanity... Sounds like either of those could net me a new skill. Tempting...

Chapter 5 I Discovered a Power That Anybody, Even an Idiot Like Me, Possesses.

It felt like ages, or like mere moments. Either way, his thoughts were spinning.

He'd sat down, watching the gem of darkness being produced and wondering what he should do.

And then the answer appeared before him.

"Sorry to keep ya waitin', sonny!" Fratello said. He had returned dressed in a long black coat.

Fratello ran over to Masato and did a little spin.

On his back was the kanji for *mom*, written upside down.

"My finest duds. The only folks who can wear this are the Four Heavenly Kings of the Libere Rebellion. Cool, right?"

"…Yeah. It is pretty cool."

Fratello was one of the Libere Heavenly Kings. The third one.

This was the Rebellion's lair.

The two figures behind Fratello peering around the edge of the door only proved it.

"Is that Masato Oosuki?"

"Whaaat? It iiiiis! Masatoooo! Heeeey!"

Amante and Sorella. They seemed mildly surprised, but not at all averse to joining them here.

Before Masato could respond, Fratello stammered, "Y'all… Ahem, you there! Why did you follow me? I specifically told you not to!"

"Who cares if you did? This is our lair—we go where we want. Also…"

"Pleeeeease, stop forcing yourself to talk like thaaaat. I know you want to be cool or whatever, but a real man would be true to himseeeelf."

"Yeah. It's not manly."

"Not manly at aaaall. Mwa-ha-haaa."

Fratello's brow twitched.

"So y'all are itchin' for a fight? Got it! ...Hey, sonny, I just gotta butcher these two numbskulls real quick. They can be kind of a pain. Mind lendin' me a hand?"

Furious, Fratello stepped up next to Masato, ready to square off against Amante and Sorella. He was eager to give them a beatdown with his new buddy.

But Masato pushed Fratello's shoulder away, rejecting it.

"...Sonny?"

"I've had enough of this farce."

"Farce? What...?"

"Don't lie to me. I already know. You and I are enemies."

"Enemies...?"

"Yeah. You're one of the Four Heavenly Kings of the Libere Rebellion. And I'm the idiot who got baited by the promise of power that would let me surpass my mother and followed you without realizing that. You really fooled me. You used me. That's what this is, right?"

Masato looked him right in the eye. And Fratello...

"The heck are you goin' on about, sonny?"

...just looked confused.

He genuinely didn't seem to know what Masato was talking about.

"No, uh...Fratello? Do you need a more detailed explanation, or...?"

"I'm thinkin' I do."

"Okay...so I'm the normal hero, Masato Oosuki. And you, Fratello, are one of the Four Heavenly Kings of the Libere Rebellion. That means we're on opposite sides. You following so far?"

"Ya lost me. Why're we enemies?"

"Huh? *That's* your question?"

Now both of them were looking confused.

Amante and Sorella stepped back, whispering to each other.

"...Uh, Sorella. You did brief Fratello on Masato Oosuki, right?"

"Huh? I thought you did thaaat. I barely consider him an enemyyyy, so I didn't say anythiiing."

"Oh, right... I didn't feel he was that important, so I don't think I even mentioned his name to Fratello at all. Probably best to keep that part quiet, huh?"

"Tooootal secrecy."

"We can hear you! So this is all your fault?!"

Masato gave the buns on Amante's head and the bone-shaped decoration on Sorella's bangs a good hard yank. ""Eek! You demon!"" "Report, inform, consult!" ""Owww!"" "Report, inform, consult!" ""We're sorry, we're sorry!"" Report, inform, and consult. The three founding principles of any functional organization.

That explained things, at least.

Masato turned back to Fratello.

"Okay, so you didn't know I was your enemy, Fratello. You didn't know that I'm Mamako Oosuki's son."

"That's news to me, sonny. So you're the infamous Mamako Oosuki's son, eh? ...Ya don't strike me as threatening or nothin', though."

"I gotta hear this from you, too?! Arghhh, fine! Well, not fine, but fine! I'm used to it, is all. Point is, you weren't actually trying to trick me, right? Right?"

Fratello nodded firmly.

"Mm. I got no reason to mess with ya. And part of this is my fault for not introducin' myself properly. Sorry 'bout that."

"I guess I could say the same thing. Which makes us even. I'm sorry, too."

"In my mind, sonny...you're a fellow man and sparring partner, one who spoke to me with his fists, our hearts as one. That fact hasn't changed."

"Oh, okay. Got it, got it. So you weren't lying. You and I are kindred spirits! Bound by the bonds between men, the perfect rivals! I wasn't wrong to believe in you!"

Masato was relieved and overjoyed.

"...Uh, Sorella? Does this mean we have to keep it a secret that Fratello's really a girl?"

"Hmm...probablyyy? Aaactually, I think it would be funnier to keep Masato in the daaark."

"Cool, I agree. So then let's make sure we don't explain that Fratello hated us so much she refused to accept that we were the same gender and started telling everyone she was a man."

"Let's keep that a seeecret."

"Like I said, we can hear— Uh...what? Huh?"

"Put a lid on it, you nitwits!"

Fratello interrupted their whispering, yanking the hair buns and bone accessory. ""Hey, you're pulling it ouuut!"" "I'm trying to." Some ripping seemed likely to occur, but Fratello couldn't care less.

"Uh, Fratello? Are you really a girl......?"

"No! These two fools are just messin' with ya. I'm a man! If ya got any doubts, do a body search! You can grope my chest and crotch all ya like!"

"Whoa, so manly! In that case..."

Masato reached a hand out.

Fratello instantly turned red and took a step back.

"...Uh."

"I-I'm a man! I don't mind if ya touch me, kid. I don't care how much my privates get fondled! But...like, you could get arrested for that, so...fair warning?"

"Glad you warned me in time then, thanks. So you *are* a girl... Okay... So literally everything I believed was wrong."

His mother, his party, his enemies, even the mysterious nun... His adventure was all girls, and the first friend he'd met who was his own gender...was just an illusion.

Masato's shoulders drooped.

"I think I get the gist of what's going on here. Regardless of whatever confusion lay between you..."

"Masato's choices played to our advaaaantage. Mwa-ha-haaa."

Amante and Sorella grinned maliciously.

"...What do you mean?"

"I'm not explaining that!" Humph!

"C'mon! This is the perfect time for it! It's your role in life!"

"It is not! I mean, when have I ever—"

"Right, riiiiight. I think it would be funnier if he knewwww? So let meeee do the honors."

The grinning Sorella summoned a giant magic tome to hover above

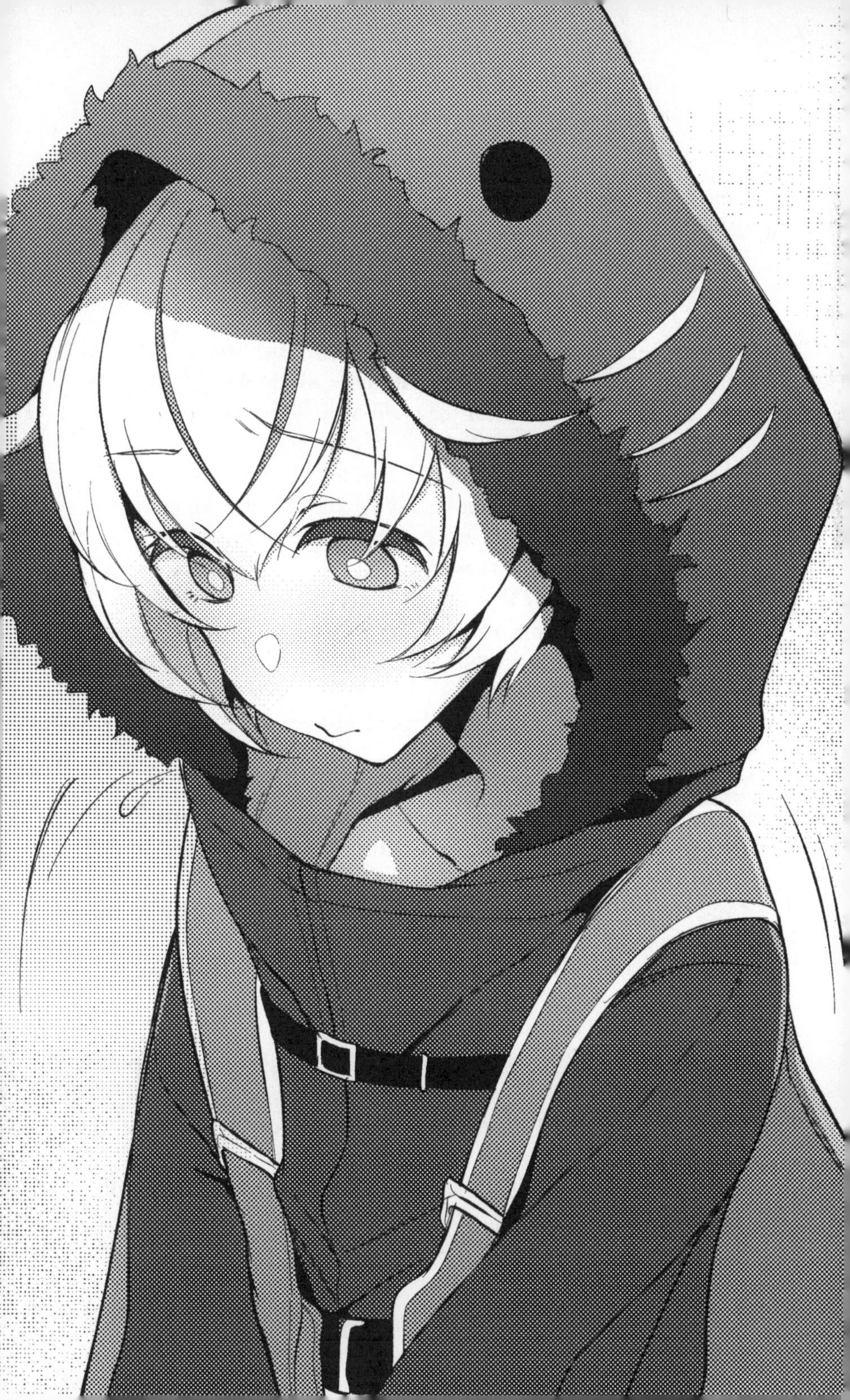

her head. The pages flipped open, and a dark light shone against the wall.

Like a projector.

"Geez! Where are we?! I guess this is where my magic—"

"Wise! Careful with the magic! There's so little room here!"

The people in the projection were in a small, dark room. Wise and Medhi were kicking the mystery-material walls, looking really frustrated. The sound made it clear they weren't holding back.

Mamako was there, too.

"I'll get this dish ready immediately! It won't take long, just you wait!"

In the center of the room was a simple kitchen, and Mamako was busy slicing daikon. *Tap, tap, tap, tap.* Rhythmically, urgently.

That was what the image showed.

"Uh…what the hell are they doing? Where is that?"

"Mamako's group came here looking for youuuu, and they ran into us insteeead. So we transported them to this lovely rooooom."

"Why'd they come here? And…what lovely room?"

"It's called The End of Moms (Eternal Housework Edition), sonny."

"Sheesh, that's long."

"First, 'The End of Moms' is part of a series of facilities the Rebellion has developed for use against mothers," explained Amante. "These rooms exist in a special realm, cut off from the world at large. So she's unable to use the power of the earth and ocean."

"And the way (Eternal Housework Edition) works iiiiis… Well, easier to show youuu. Come heeere."

He looked closer…

Inside the room known as The End of Moms (Eternal Housework Edition).

While Wise and Medhi were angrily kicking the wall, Mamako was busy cooking.

She had the daikon all chopped to bite-sized pieces and was boiling them in some dashi in a pot.

She skimmed the scum off the top, added some miso, adjusted the seasonings…and it was all done!

"Hee-hee. Just the way I like it! I'm sure Ma-kun will be happy."

"You're done, Mamako?"

"Then somewhere…!"

Their eyes darted along the walls.

A door in the wall to Wise's left slid open.

"This way! Come on!"

All three went through the door and down a narrow passage to another small room.

"Another room! Argh, I'm so pissed!"

"And more of the same."

This room was the same size as the last, with walls and a floor of the same material.

But this time, there was a pile of laundry in the center.

And a threatening message: WE HAVE YOUR CHILD. IF YOU WANT THEM BACK, YOU, THE MOTHER, MUST FOLD ALL THIS LAUNDRY.

Mamako immediately knelt down and began folding.

"Okay! I'll get this taken care of, and we can go find Ma-kun!"

"Wait, don't, Mamako! This is definitely messed up!"

"There were clothes four rooms ago, and eight rooms ago… It's on a cycle. Cleaning, laundry, cooking, folding…we're just looping through the same four tasks."

"Yes, I did notice… Okay, all done!"

With ruthless efficiency, she'd cleared the requirement.

The wall to Mamako's right opened, and a passage appeared. "Let's go!" "Hey! Mamako!" "Wait!" Mamako was already gone.

And they found themselves in another small room. This time there were a broom, a pile of dust, and a rag and bucket.

Another threatening note.

WE HAVE YOUR CHILD. IF YOU WANT THEM BACK, YOU, THE MOTHER, MUST CLEAN THIS ROOM.

"Let's get started! Time to clean!"

"Absolutely not! Mamako, calm down! This is obviously a trap! Clearing these tasks isn't getting us any closer to Masato!"

Wise's desperate cry made Mamako's hand pause an inch above the rag.

But only for a moment. She was soon wiping the floor.

"Perhaps you're right about that, Wise. But I can feel it. I can feel us getting close to Ma-kun."

"No, but…"

"Even if that's true, keeping this up is a bad idea. This is clearly a trap. A trap designed to make you do indefinite housework and wear yourself out! So…"

"Yes. It might well be a trap, Medhi. I'm just doing ordinary house-work, but I can feel it sapping my strength."

"Then…!"

"But I'm not going to stop. There's always a chance it isn't a trap."

She dunked the rag in the bucket and firmly wrung it out.

Pausing only to wipe a drop of sweat from her cheek, Mamako began wiping the floor.

"I'm fine. I'm fine. I'm a mother. If it's for my child, I can do any-thing. No matter how hard it is, I can keep going. Because I'm a mother. So leave this to me. I'm fine."

Imagining the moment when she and her child were reunited, she smiled happily.

And so she set to work, sweat beading on her brow.

Masato couldn't drag his eyes away from the projection of Mamako.

"You're clearly *not* fine… For the love of… Stop it. Please," he mut-tered, half in disbelief, half in anger.

Although honestly, neither was his primary emotion. Despite him-self, he could feel heat building at the edges of his eyes.

But fortunately, the tone-deaf crowd around him distracted him before the tears could flow.

"Oh myyyy… Wise and Medhi figured it ouuuut… But too baaaad! Mamako's fallen for it hook, line, and siiiinker."

"Of course! The more a mother cares for her child, the more ines-capable this trap becomes! She'll be trapped in an infinite loop of instructions until she destroys herself! Heh-heh-heh!"

"Hold it. Watching her destroy herself sounds real dull. We should free her eventually. Do none of y'all want to beat Mamako Oosuki yourselves? Know what I mean, sonny?"

Fratello had run over to Masato and was tugging at his sleeve.

"Sonny, we should start training now! We'll get ya nice and strong, and then you can use that strength to butcher Mamako Oosuki! Right?!"

Fratello was all excited, like she was inviting Masato to play.

But Masato slapped her hand away.

"...Sonny?"

"I finally worked it out. I know what kind of power I want."

Without so much as a glance at Fratello's stunned face, Masato started walking.

He drew Firmamento, held it tight, and stood before the projection of Mamako.

"...Mom, I finally understand."

The image of his mother desperately trying to save her son had helped him figure it out.

To Masato, *power* meant...

"The thing you need to save who you want to save...that's what power is."

Even now, he still couldn't just say *to save my mother*, so he still had a long way to go. But inside, he understood.

Masato raised his sword, drawing it back all the way behind him.

"Great Heavens... You who have stood by as Mother Earth and Mother Ocean produced one thing after another... You stood by, as I did... So you know how I feel... You know what I want to do. Yes! This is our time! Lend me your power!" he roared in supplication.

Certain he could do it.

"Wh-what?! What's Masato Oosuki doing?!"

"I dunnooooo! But he's sure fired uuuup!"

"Sonny... No way... Is this some special power?!"

The Heavenly Kings gasped, frozen in place, watching...

As Masato unleashed...

"Ultimate Secret Art...Spacetime Slash!"

He swung Firmamento with all his might!

The Ultimate Secret Art: Spacetime Slash—the most powerful blow the hero chosen by the heavens could muster! An ultimate move made possible by his daily training and his desire to save you-know-who!

The slash cut through the wall between realms, freeing his trapped party members!

"Oh, it opened! Cool, we're out!"

That was the real Wise talking! Not the projection!

It came from waaaaay behind Masato.

"...Huh? Behind me?"

The wall in front of Masato hadn't budged. Instead, the wall behind him had slid open, allowing the girls to step out.

"So...uh..."

"Sonny, your ultimate move sliced space-time!"

"R-right! Let's say it did!"

"They came out somewhere totally unrelated to the place you were looking! Are these super-dimensional forces at work?!"

"P-probably... No, definitely! Exactly what I was trying to do!"

"Aaaand...you slashed horizontallyyyy...not verticallyyyy...but the wall parted right and leeeeft. You can control the direction of the cut at wiiiill? That's amaaaazing."

"I know, right? That's totally what happened! I'm incredible! I have finally awakened...!"

Then his party's voices followed:

"I guess the trap just gave up, huh? That's our Mamako!"

"She ran them out of laundry, ingredients, and places that needed cleaning! Hats off to Mamako's housework power."

"I'm just glad it worked out! Hee-hee."

Oh well.

Amante, Sorella, even Fratello all just stared at Masato in silence.

Yep.

"Uh...I was all like, 'Wonder if I can do this? It'd be cool if I could'... but sorry, I guess that was all in my head."

He wasn't going to cry. Men don't cry. Masato apologized properly and put his sword away.

He put the entire incident behind him, acting like nothing had happened. He greeted his party with a smile.

"Hey, Mom! Everyone! Been ages! Glad you're safe—!"

"Yeah, yeah, we'll save the heartfelt reunions for later. Along with the lecture for being stupid enough to go off with the enemy."

"First, we have to deal with the Heavenly Kings…but before that, Masato, you have work to do."

"Huh? I do?"

"Ma-kun! There you are! Mommy was so worried!"

"*Gasp!* Here she comes!"

The moment her gaze found Masato, Mamako broke into a run.

Driven by the sheer power of worry for her child, she swept him into a hug, nuzzled fiercely until she could relax. And so Masato's "job" was fulfilled.

In theory.

"Step back."

But before Mamako could reach him, Fratello stepped between them, placing her hand on Mamako's belly. An instant later, her body was flung away.

"Eek…?!"

"Mom?!"

She was flung toward the stone pedestal where the dark gem was forming.

"Oh crap! No time for a defense spell!"

"Then we'll have to—!"

Before Mamako hit the pedestal, Wise and Medhi physically flung themselves behind her. "Unh?!" "Oof!" With the two of them cushioning her—and getting crushed by the impact—Mamako avoided major damage.

"Wise? Medhi?! S-s-sorry!"

"D-don't worry about it… We rely on you all the time."

"I'm glad we could be of help. More importantly…"

The impact had shaken the pedestal, and the unnatural vibrations had activated a safety device.

A magic cage had appeared around the pedestal, trapping Mamako and the girls within.

"My magic can take care of this! …*Spara la magia per mirare… Bomba Sfera!* …Huh? My magic isn't working?!"

"Tough luck, y'all. Magic don't work inside that there cage. Mom power don't work, neither."

"Good news, Wise! This isn't your usual personal tragedy!" cheered Medhi.

"Whew, thank goodness… Wait, no! This is terrible! We just got out of one trap, and here we are in another! It's not fair! Arghhh!"

"This is extremely unpleasant, you're right… I'm so depressed…!"

Wise and Medhi (dark version) seized the bars of the magic cage, rattling them with all their might.

Amante and Sorella watched with delight.

"Ah-ha-ha! This is perfect for you! Why not change jobs to Wild Animal? Then a circus could take you in! That would be even better!"

"Getting caught twice in a rooooow? That's sooooo dumb. Pathetiiic! Stiiiill…Mamako seriously managed to beat The End of Moms rooooom?"

"Good point. Did (Eternal Housework Edition) really run out of supplies? We'd better go check."

Amante and Sorella stepped into the trap room.

The door in the wall snapped shut behind them. Nothing of it remained in their wake.

The projection on the other wall showed Amante and Sorella frantically pounding the wall for a while, but then the giant magic tome vanished, taking the projection with it.

"Where in the heck does their stupidity end…?" Fratello grumbled.

But then she gasped, sensing an unnatural presence behind her.

"……Whew……"

With that small sigh, Masato stepped forward past Fratello, who watched was watching him intently.

He reached the cage and spoke to his trapped companions.

"You both okay?"

"We're not okay! We're stuck in here! Wait… Uh, Masato?"

"We've taken some damage, but it's not exactly fatal… Um…Masato?"

Wise and Medhi both saw the oddly peaceful look on his face and trailed off.

"Um…Masato? You *are* Masato, right?"

"You seem really different…"

"I'm me. No one else."

Having checked on them, next…

He turned his eyes to Mamako, sitting behind them, covered in sweat again.

"Mom. Are you okay?"

"Yes! Mommy's fine! Just fine! And now that I've found you, Ma-kun, Mommy feels so, so great…!"

"Right, right. You're lying."

"I…I'm not—"

"You are."

He calmly met her gaze, and she fell silent.

"…Mom, we need to talk."

"Y-yes? What is it?"

Surprised, Mamako shifted herself, sitting upright on her knees.

Like she thought he was going to scold her. He was.

Perhaps for the first time in his life. There was a weird anger in his voice.

"Mom, you always say you're fine no matter what… Don't do that!"

"Huh? …B-but I am fine, so—"

"When you really are fine, that's okay. But stop saying you're fine when you aren't fine. Mom, you can use all these crazy-strong powers and do almost anything…but even you get tired sometimes."

"Well…certainly, but—"

"But when that happens, you lie about it and insist you're doing fine, which just makes me even more worried. Mom, do you like making me worried?"

"I—I don't, no! Mommy was trying to keep you from worrying. That's why—"

"Well, if the result is that I worry even more, then that's the wrong approach. Right?"

They stared at each other for a long moment, and then Mamako hung her head.

"That's…fair enough. You're right."

"So think about it, okay? Consider what's the best thing to do in that moment. I might always be your son, but…but maybe sometimes, I can actually help you."

"Ma-kun…"

"So, um…my point is…I worry about you the same way you worry about me. And I'd appreciate it if you could bear that in mind. The end."

It was a son's duty to speak his mind clearly.

Mamako stared at her hands, but a smile played across her lips.

"That's right…you do worry about Mommy, Ma-kun. Hee-hee."

Her body was starting to glow. "Don't get happy about this!"

"S-sorry." He was midlecture here.

But his feelings were actually getting through. Well, he hoped so anyway.

"Okay, Mom. Be honest. Are you tired right now?"

"…Yes, I am a little tired."

"Then rest there a minute. You don't need to do a thing. This time, I'm gonna save you for real."

Mamako nodded.

"Okay. I'll sit right here and rest. Mommy won't do a thing."

"Wise, Medhi, you guys rest, too. And watch over Mom for me. I'll take care of the rest."

"Uh, okay…sure… Whatever you say."

"Very well. The rest is up to you, Masato."

Both girls sat down, staring at him transfixed, like they'd never seen him before.

Mamako leaned back against the pillar, resting.

Immediately, the special mom skill A Mother's Day Off activated!

Like the name suggested, this gave mothers a time to rest. If their children were looking after them, they had no choice but to do nothing. It was a mandatory rest.

And the effect of it went through Mamako's back to the pedestal, from the pedestal down the cords, down the cords to the magic circle on the floor…

…and reached the gel sphere placed in the center of that circle, stopping the data transfer.

The creation of the dark gem was halted completely.

"Hey, uh…I think Mamako just did something?"

"By *not* doing anything…"

"Ma-kun! Don't worry about Mommy, Ma-kun! I'll just rest right here, not doing anything! Hee-hee!"

"Seriously? Even when you're doing nothing? …Geez. My mom will always be my mom."

She waved happily at him, and he couldn't help but smile back.

Then he turned to face the girl he'd believed to be his kindred spirit.

With his party watching over him from behind, Masato faced Fratello down.

Fratello's dazed eyes were gazing up at him reproachfully.

"…A man like yourself, actin' like that in front of his mother? It don't make no sense."

"What makes no sense?"

"If you wanna lecture her, do it with your fists! That's the manly way! Men make their mothers submit!"

"That's not called 'being a man.' That's called 'being a piece of shit.'"

"No, it ain't!"

"It is."

They glared at each other for a moment. Then Masato sighed and drew his sword.

"You mean," he said, "that's your source of power."

"It is! Mine is the power to butcher mothers! That's the power ya wanted, sonny!"

"Thanks for the offer, but I'm gonna have to decline. That's not what I wanted. I don't need power like that."

Fratello pouted, looking grumpy.

"…You get on with your mother, sonny? You wanna get all huggy and kissy?"

"Of course not. I just wanna have a decently fun adventure with her in a totally normal way, like normal families do."

"That's crazy talk."

"Maybe. It feels like that sometimes. She's always with me and always better than me. She often leaves me without a leg to stand on. I've lost count of how many times that's made me feel super depressed. But at the same time, the crazy stuff is kinda fun. Like, it's so crazy, there's no way anyone could get through it...and that's why I want to try to get through it myself."

"Utter madness, I tell ya."

"That's fine with me. An adventure through the heart of madness... what man doesn't get pumped up by that?"

He gave Fratello a mocking grin.

Disgusted, Fratello sighed.

And looked up at Masato as if facing a mortal enemy.

"If that's your word as a man, I won't argue with ya. I'm a man, too. I know what it means when your mind's made up."

"Glad to hear it. And yeah, my mind *is* made up. And while I'm at it...I've had enough of this."

He pointed his blade at Fratello.

"Fratello...how dare you do that to my Mom?!"

All the anger he'd been suppressing as he tried to keep himself calm exploded out of him.

Masato slashed sideways, aiming directly for Fratello's throat.

"Mah!"

Fratello leaped high, avoiding it.

Right where Masato wanted her.

"Perfect! I'll finish this in a single blow! Rahhhh!"

He put all his strength into a single swing of Firmamento.

Unleashing a shock wave of anger right at Fratello.

"Good attack, but not good enough, sonny!"

Right before the shock wave hit her, Fratello rolled, twisting herself in midair.

The second her feet hit the ground, she closed the gap between them.

"Mah!"

"Too obvious!"

Fratello's trademark straight punch. Masato held out his left arm.

The shield wall deployed, and the instant it caught the fist, there was a dull clunk.

For a moment, he saw a bunch of metal bits, like brass knuckles. They swiftly pulled back into Fratello's sleeve, out of sight.

"...You've got some weird weapon there, huh?"

"I have a fisticuffs weapon equipped. I put these on my arms and punch, and they come flying out."

"I see. So you're a master of hidden weapons."

"They're just ordinary weapons. My sleeves are just too long, makin' 'em hard to see. I'm not actually tryin' to hide 'em."

"Right... It did seem out of character."

"Also, while I'm at it, my attacks are super-powerful against mothers, but they're just regular ol' punches against anyone else. But with these weapons equipped, I might get extraordinary attacks even against normal opponents."

"Like a lucky crit? Well, I appreciate the fair and up-front explanation."

"You're welcome."

Fratello came in close again. But she wasn't unnaturally fast like Amante. Masato kept calm, watching...

And stuck out his left arm just as her fist came out. Shield wall. "Mah!" "Humph!" He easily caught the cluster of brass knuckles that shot out of the sleeve. One-handed.

"Too bad! Missed me!"

"It'll hit next time! Mahhhh!"

Fratello lowered her hips, straining every muscle, charging, preparing for the ultimate blow that had sent the mountain-sized horned from flying and carved a hole in the forest.

If that gets a lucky crit, it'll be real bad... Should I dodge? ...Nope! I'm soaking it!

Masato wanted to deny Fratello's best blow head-on.

So he stood his ground.

"Come at me, Fratello!"

"Prepare yourself, sonny! Mah!"

Fratello's ultimate fist! Masato deployed his shield wall!

And easily caught it.

"Tch, another whiff!" Fratello cursed.

"Back at you!"

Masato swung his Holy Sword down…!

"Mah!"

Fratello put both her hands above her head, eyes squeezed tightly closed, a desperate defense. A super-cute little girl guard!

If Masato attacked that, he would definitely, unquestionably, look like the bad guy.

He hastily stopped his swing.

"Hey! That's cheating!"

"What, you ain't gonna attack? Then I will! Mah!"

"You know, that cute little squeak you do is actually pretty cheap, too! Argh!"

He caught Fratello's fist on his shield wall again.

And this time Masato's attack—!

"Mah!" Girly guard!

"I said, stop that! Please!!"

"What, pullin' your blow again? Then I guess I'll attack! Mah!"

"Arghhh! This is really tough… Er…"

He was trying to block, but his shield wall was being pushed back.

And not just pushed back. His shield wall shattered, and a little fist broke through. The moment it touched Masato's gut…

Masato was flung back, hard.

"Gah…?!"

All the way back, no time to catch himself. He slammed hard into the wall.

The girls all leaped to their feet.

"Oh no! Ma-kun?!"

"H-hey, what the heck? Medhi, let's get in there!"

"Yes! I just need to cast a healing spell—!"

"This is my fight! Stay out of it!" Masato roared.

The girls all froze.

Honestly, this was rough. His back was on fire. He was in tremendous pain. All the air had been forced out of his lungs, and his chest hurt. If he didn't get healed, he would be in trouble. He knew that well enough.

But he *had* to finish this himself.

Some things I need to finish alone!

As a hero… As a man… In full knowledge that it was foolish pride.

Obeying the impulse that had risen up when he saw his mother get blown away.

He had to get payback. No matter what.

Ignoring the pain, Masato got up and raised his sword.

Fratello cracked her knuckles menacingly as she strode forward.

"You sure you don't wanna beg your li'l ol' mommy to save you?"

"Yeah. Can't have you unleashing a 'Don't go crying to Mommy, brah' instant death attack, can I?"

"A what now?"

"Never mind."

"Hmm… But fair enough. I'm all warmed up. I can really strut my stuff. You ready, sonny?"

"I've always been ready. Come at me."

They faced each other from midrange.

Fratello pulled her right fist back, charging it. Preparing for a devastating blow. Charging, charging, charging…

The power was now so concentrated the air around them was shaking.

But part of Masato still wanted to believe in his kindred spirit. So he asked, "Hey, why is it you're so big on…*butchering*, was it?"

"Butchering, yep."

"Why butcher mothers? What makes you do that? You got something against them? I mean, not like I'm totally unsympathetic, but… Well?" he asked.

But Fratello just gave him a glazed look.

"No real reason."

"…Huh?"

"I've got this here power that's only good against mothers, so I'm usin' it. If I'm against a mother, I can win every time. Winning's fun. That's all."

"What the…? You've got nothing against them, but because you know you can win, you turned violent? You just want to beat people up? …Just like a kid acting out in their rebellious phase."

"Not kid! Man!"

"You ain't a man, though, physically or psychologically. You're way off the mark. Geez. *Sigh...* I really picked all the wrong things to believe, huh? This is a disaster. Dammit."

He was so frustrated with himself that he felt like giving up, but he endured.

"Makes you want to stop trying to believe in things, but...I'm gonna choose to believe anyway."

Masato raised his sword.

"To protect my mom...and other mothers...I can't let an idiot like you run wild. I believe I have the power to do that!"

Putting his emotions into words helped him focus.

And his focus caused a change in Firmamento. The translucent blade began filling with specks of light.

Like glittering stars tracing a Milky Way through the blade.

"This is... Oh, I see... At last, you're willing to help. Thanks, partner. Me and my powers of protection will defeat you, Fratello!"

"Mm. Then my powers of destruction will cut them down!"

Both leaped forward.

"Rahhhhhhhhhhhh!"

"Mahhhhh!"

A swing and a thrust clashed together.

Aura sparkling around it, Fratello's fist touched the sword. The power charged within tried to blow the sword and Masato away, but...

The protective power soaked that thrust, deflecting it.

"Mah...?!"

"I win. Here's what you get in place of a lecture, you dumb kid."

The flat of his powerful blade struck Fratello's head.

Fratello's eyes rolled up until the whites were visible, and she fell flat on her face.

The fight was over.

Fratello was completely unconscious.

Certain his foe was out of commission, Masato turned to the cage trapping his party and raised his blade.

"I'll get you guys out of there. I have the power now! This time it'll work! Ultimate Secret Art…!"

The ultimate move of a hero who'd awakened to his true power. An ultimate slash so powerful the space-time continuum ceased to matter. Magic cages were no match for it…

But before he could unleash it, Wise and Medhi pushed the bars out of the way one-handed and stepped out.

"Oh, that was easy. How'd that happen?"

"That was most likely because of Mamako's skill A Mother's Day Off. The ability to keep us inside is on vacation."

"Cool."

Oh well. His party was already free. "But…I was about to… Oh, never mind." Masato put his sword away, muttering.

Wise and Medhi came hustling right over to him.

"Geez, Masato! Are you okay?"

"Let me treat those wounds! Then we'll talk!"

"Calm down, you two. I'm fine. I took a fair bit of damage, but my equipment has an auto-heal, so my HP's recovering just fine."

"That's *not* what I meant!"

Both girls put their hands on his forehead.

"Have you lost it completely?!"

"Why is *that* your concern?"

"You haven't been behaving like yourself at all!" said Medhi. "Getting mad on your mother's behalf? Obtaining the power to protect mothers? Winning a one-on-one duel with one of the Four Heavenly Kings?!"

"You were, like, actually kinda cool?! Like, for real! Even though you're Masato! And that's impossible! So how can we not be worried?!"

"Have you guys ever thought of giving me *non*-backhanded compliments."

"We could do that, but we're too worried!"

"Right, okay, sorry to worry everyone, geez. Still…"

Masato braced himself, pretty sure it was high time Mamako came over for a hug.

She didn't.

"…Oh my…what is this? Something feels so strange…"

She was still sitting on the pedestal, looking around nervously, like she just couldn't stay calm.

"What's she doing? Eh, doesn't matter."

It wasn't like he wanted a reward hug. Really, he didn't!

Anyway…

"Uh, right. Point is, you two shouldn't be worried about me. Gimme some space, okay? There's something I gotta do."

"What?"

"This is where they make the gems of darkness. See that giant blobby sphere in the middle? That's the source. Best way to protect this world is to destroy that thing and make sure they can never use it again."

"There you go again, Masato, acting like a real hero! …Wise!"

"I know! I gotta chain cast until his head gets back on straight!"

"I've had enough of you both."

Taking a tight grip on his sword, Masato stepped toward the gel sphere alone.

But then…darkness burst upward in front of Masato, swirling around.

"Wh-what the heck is that?"

"Nothing you need to know about. Just shut up and listen." An unfathomable voice echoed from within the swirl. "My plans cannot proceed. I am displeased. Extremely displeased. And you're the cause. This is your fault! You just had to be here."

"Our fault…?"

"And the root cause must be punished. Submit to my power and lose all that you have built. Sink to the bottom of the sea along with these failures who cannot follow orders."

And with what sounded like a curse, the swirl vanished.

Everything around them began to shake. It felt like the floor fell a few feet. Everyone dropped to their knees.

"Wh-what is this? What's happening?"

"What did that creepy swirl do? Masato, explain!"

"Uh, I have no idea."

"Ma-kun! Above you!"

"Huh?"

Masato looked up and saw a piece of the ceiling collapsing. One that was definitely big enough to kill him if it hit his head. "Seriously?!" He dived sideways, barely avoiding it.

Mamako came running over, lurching with the floor's shakes.

"Ma-kun, are you hurt?"

"N-no, I'm fine! Thanks! We've gotta get outta here, though! Fast!"

"Yes! Let's do that… Oh, wait, Ma-kun! We have to make sure those other children get out, too!"

"Do we have time to worry about them?"

"They'll be just fine."

The walls leading to The End of Moms (Eternal Housework Edition) opened, and Hahako stepped out with laundry and rags in hand and Amante and Sorella—looking exhausted—under each arm.

"Hahako?! You're here, too?!"

"I just had a bad feeling. I was right to come check on them. I'll take care of things here. Can I leave the rest to you, Mamako?"

"Certainly! I'll take care of Ma-kun and the girls! I'm supposed to be resting, but this is an emergency, so I think it'll be okay!"

"Well, then… Until we meet again."

Mamako and Hahako exchanged smiles. Hahako levitated smoothly over to Fratello, scooped her up, said, "This one's a third potential child!" and sank into the floor carrying all three Heavenly Kings.

"Thank goodness Hahako arrived! …Well, then, Ma-kun!"

"Yeah! Let's evac!"

"Yeah…but, uh, where from?"

"Is there an exit?"

"I can infooorm you that there's one this way! As sure as my name is Shiraaase!"

Someone was standing in the room's main entrance, waving. Even in a moment like this, she wouldn't drop her shtick—that was definitely the real Shiraaase.

"Porta already evacuated! Hurry!"

"Right, let's run for it!"

The violent shaking was causing more pieces of the ceiling to fall. One hit the dark gem creation sphere, shattering it. A pillar toppled, smashing the gem on the pedestal. Destruction rained down upon them from all directions.

Keeping one eye above them, staggering each time the floor beneath their feet dropped, they scrambled as fast as they could toward the door.

Outside the lair was the cave-like tunnel. It branched in all directions, but there was a stuffed animal placed at every fork to indicate the way forward.

Following this adorable guide, they made it up the tunnel and outside to a spectacular view of the island.

And to someone even cuter than the stuffed animals, hopping up and down and waving.

"Masatoooo! Over here!"

"Oh, there's Porta! Glad you're safe!"

The party was back together. Ideally, that would mean they were in the clear…

But being outside just meant they could stop worrying about the ceiling falling. The ground itself was still shaking and lurching downward.

And they discovered something even more concerning.

"Um, Ma-kun…does it seem like the island is getting smaller?"

"It's not getting smaller…it's sinking. The entire island is sinking!"

From up here they could tell the beach was already gone. As the island sank, the water rolled in, covering the island. The pier was totally gone, the water cottages half-submerged. And the dinghies on the beach must have drifted away—there were no boats in sight.

The border between land and sea was moving steadily closer. The tourists were fleeing, headed inland.

This was causing congestion on the promenade. The shopping area had so many luggage-toting tourists trying to escape that it looked ready to burst. Nobody could move at all.

"Hey! Up here! You've got to get higher!"

"Wise, wait! Even if they climb up here, that might not help!"

"What do you mean, Medhi? Better than nothing!"

"Perhaps, but if we don't solve the core problem—"

"Settle down, you two. No time for arguing. Let's all take a deep breath and try to figure out a solution. If we rela—auuugh, it sank again!"

The only way they could stay upright was by clinging to one another. Mamako had her arms tight around Masato, refusing to let go. Wise and Medhi were holding each other close, even as they bickered. Porta had frantically clapped her arms around Shiraaase. How could anyone stay calm...?

Well, Shiraaase was. She always was.

"The underlying structure of the island is being deleted, step-by-step. So this why we were told to evacuate..."

"Shiraaase? What do you mean?"

"Earlier, I had a chance to speak with the mastermind behind the Rebellion. We were given a warning. They're likely the cause of our current predicament."

"The Rebellion mastermind? I suppose this weird swirly thing did show up and tell us we'd lose everything we'd built and sink to the bottom of the sea... Was that the mastermind?"

"A black swirl? Absolutely. They're attempting to destroy evidence and interfere with our investigation, as well as get revenge on you. Although perhaps this is more a fit of jealousy... Well, there are many potential reasons. It's most troubling."

"That's putting it mildly! But we'll have to discuss that later! First..."

The island was sinking. People were fleeing. What should they do?

"I've got an idea!" Wise cried. "We can use transport magic!"

"That might save us, but what about all these tourists?" said Medhi. "You don't have the MP or the time to transport all of them!"

"Then admin powers... Oh, no good. This server's world was just opened and the admin cheat moves haven't been implemented yet... which means..."

Before Shiraaase could even say her name, Mamako let go of Masato and ran over to Porta.

"Porta, dear, can I have my swords?"

"O-okay! I'll get them!"

"Mom, what are you...?"

"Ma-kun, don't worry. You let me have a nice rest, and I'm feeling much better. So I think I can give this a good shot."

Practically speaking, the only thing that could salvage this situation was Mamako's power. She'd caused plenty of miracles before, and seemingly nothing was impossible for her... They had to place their faith in her abilities once more.

And this was no time to insist she not push herself. Masato swallowed his concern and his frustrations and nodded.

"Thank you, Ma-kun. Well, then..."

The Holy Sword of Mother Earth was in her right hand, that of Mother Ocean in her left.

Raising both swords high, Mamako prayed.

"Great motherly powers, please... I want to save everyone who's in danger... Please, lend me your power!"

And the desire to save everyone was heard.

The waves threatening to swallow the stragglers stopped.

And the jungle began to move.

The giant broccoli stalks split of their own accord, slicing themselves into planks and building themselves into ships. Vines bound the planks together, securing everything. A massive volume of leaves filled the little gaps...

It was a massive ark, big enough to carry an entire city!

"Whoaaaa! Mamako, you did it again!"

"Excellent work! From now on, we're changing your name to Noah."

"My mom doesn't need an even weirder name. Still...Mom did it again. *Sigh.*"

"Next, let's get all the tourists on board... O-oh?"

Mamako's knees suddenly buckled. "Ah!" Masato quickly caught her, and they avoided a complete disaster...

...but Mamako was covered in sweat and breathing heavily.

"Hey, Mom! Are you... No, you're clearly not okay!"

"S-sorry... I feel a little dizzy... I guess I'm still tired. Oh my! This is bad!"

The moment the power left Mamako, the waves started rising again.

The ark was near the entrance to the promenade, and the waves lapped at it. It was already starting to drift.

"Eep!" cried Porta. "The ship's gonna wash away!"

"Can we control the waves and bring it this way...? No, not an option," said Shiraaase. "Mamako's too tired. She doesn't have the strength left."

"Uh, Masato! This is bad! Real bad!"

"You've got to do something, Masato!"

"R-right! Leave it to me! I have the power now!"

Propping up Mamako up with one arm, Masato pulled his sword with the other, focusing.

The blade filled with stars, and his body with power.

And that was all.

"Dammit! Something happen! I've got people to protect! My power has to protect all of these people! Let me do it!"

But no matter how long he waited, a Mamako-style miracle did not occur.

"Masato, Masato. It'll never do to go on about protecting people. That's completely out of character. You sound ridiculous."

"Shiraaase?! This isn't a time to make fun of me!"

"No, no. That's not my intent. I'm trying to clear up your confusion."

"Confusion?"

"Remember what is most important in this world. What this world requires of you, a Normal Hero. If you can work that out, a miracle will happen."

The most important thing in this world was the bonds between parents and children.

What was required of a Normal Hero wasn't the power to save the world. What Masato was supposed to strive for as a Normal Hero was to become close to his mother in a normal way and to live a normal, happy life.

When I fought Fratello…I thought, this is for my Mom. And then the strength…

He remembered now.

"Goodness, it's so bright! …Oh my! Ma-kun's sword!"

"…Huh?"

Firmamento's blade had gone from specks of light to a full-on glow. A gentle glow, like moonlight.

"Oh! Looks like a power-up! Right on! Now my power can cause a miracle…"

Or so he thought, but suddenly the sword's light went out. "Huhhh?!" He must have messed up.

Or maybe...

"Um, Holy Sword? Great Heavens? This can't be right, but...does it only work if it's related to mothers? Like, if I ask if you can help my mom, you'll lend me your power? That it?"

The moment he asked...

Firmamento glowed as bright as the sun, unleashing incredible power.

The glow illuminated the entire island, and every tourist bathed in that light began to levitate. Swept safely into the sky, every last one was carried toward the ark.

Then all the island's buildings lifted up. The cottages, the hotel, the shops, even Mamako's statue. Everything Mamako had labored to build for the children's pleasure was packed onto the ark as well.

And so was Masato's party.

"Whoa! We're floating, too! We're flying! This is amazing!" Porta squealed.

"This power activated when Masato thought hard about Mamako," Shiraaase explained. "In other words, this power is derived from Mamako. We're being saved by proxy! Heh-heh-heh."

"That's how Masato always does things! Whew! What a relief."

"And that's just how Masato should be. All's right in the world. Thank goodness."

Porta and Shiraaase bobbed along, while Wise and Medhi broke out their best crawl, the entire party happily swimming through the air toward the ark.

If everyone was having fun, that was best...except for one poor dejected soul.

"My power only works if it's for my mom... What kind of power is that...? *Sigh...*"

This was not the power Masato had hoped for.

"We've all been saved because of you, Ma-kun. Thank you!"

"...Yeah, you're welcome."

His mother's smiling face was too close. He turned his head away.

But the chosen hero/son had to admit it wasn't the worst feeling in the world.

The Hero Masato Oosuki's Ultimate Move Development 5

Mom, you're pretty much always throwing around ultimate skills. You don't, like, picture something in your mind when you attack, right?

MAMAKO

Let me see. When I'm fighting, I never think about anything except keeping you and the girls out of danger.

So that's the secret to your power... No hope for me, then.

MAMAKO

I don't think that's true. I'm sure you can do it, Ma-kun. Why not train a little with Mommy?

If it gets me an ultimate move, then, yeah, maybe that's an option...

MAMAKO

So, to make sure I have plenty of time to train with you, let me just go defeat all the enemies and beat this game in a jiffy!

Yeah, make quick work of it... Wait, if you do that, there's no point! Stop!!

Epilogue

The new beastkin area, Materland. Far to the south of the starting point in Materville was one of this world's few resort areas.

Lapped at by the warm southern seas, the island was a paradise. Sun, sea, sand, and colorful tropical flowers. Play, eat, and rest to your heart's content. A luxurious vacation meeting all your needs.

Here are the island's most popular attractions:

In third place, beastkin beach volleyball. Women boasting animal ears, tails, and astounding athletic physiques using their species' famously high stats to trounce one another's teams with a ball made of solid stone. Whipping beastkin audiences into a frenzy, this was less a sport and more a martial art.

In second, the beastkin fire dance show. Muscular beastkin in grass skirts wielding fire, breathing fire, setting themselves alight and emerging unscathed—a vastly entertaining spectacle.

And the current most popular attraction…

"Oh, look! The ship the heroes made! Gosh, it's so big!"

"They used it to escape some island… I wonder which island…"

"Rumor has it the island grew popular overnight and then suddenly sank into the ocean. It's a legendary island!"

"Like, super legendary. And it has some rare items the heroes accidentally dropped! A treasure hunter's dream!"

The majestic ark in the harbor was currently drawing the bulk of the tourists.

A ship the size of an island itself, with a hotel and plenty of shops on board. At the prow, a goddess-like statue of Mamako. A ship under the protection of Mothers Ocean and Earth, guaranteed safe passage.

And the one who built the ship had deemed it be named the SS *Thank You For Helping, Ma-kun*. The name was inscribed on the ship's side, gleaming proudly in the sunlight.

So...

On the beach.

"...Huh? The Rebellion Elimination Plan?"

Masato had been sprawled out on the beach trying not to scowl at the ark, but this got him on his feet.

He was surrounded by Mamako, Porta, Wise, Medhi, and Shiraaase, all lounging on beach chairs in their swimsuits.

Mountains, plateau, plateau, hills, and hills. But all boob topography aside...

The hills farthest away from Masato were the ones that mattered now—Shiraaase's hills.

"That plan was why you came? You were running that the whole time? This is the first I've heard of it..."

"I infooormed you of it."

"You were so obsessed with Fratello you didn't bother listening. We all heard her."

"The events on that island and the operation itself are considered complete with the sinking of their lair. All you need understand is that it's over."

"Uh, okay...sure...then, um...good work, everyone?"

Some major goals had been accomplished without his knowledge. That was cool! And sort of mortifying. Masato ended up on his knees, repenting.

Shiraaase shot him a thin smile...but it soon faded.

"But there is one related matter I must infooorm you of," she said, glancing around the party.

Medhi seemed to catch her hint and sat up.

"Porta, would you like to go swimming with me? Wise, you stay here."

"Okay! I'll join you!!"

"Why are you leaving me out?" whined Wise. "I wanna come, too!"

The three girls ran off toward the surf, playing at the water's edge. A sight to behold.

Although Masato was a little disappointed that they hadn't asked him to join them.

"Masato, you should be panting after a MILF like me, not those children. This infooormation is serious."

"That statement is pretty much the opposite of serious...but sorry. Go ahead."

"Following the operation to destroy the Rebellion's lair, we're currently attempting to suppress the mastermind behind everything. This relates to that plan..."

"...How so?"

"This plan will require your party's assistance. Thoroughly, from start to finish, and undivided. You will find yourselves at the center of it without me lifting a finger to put you there. Understood?"

"Seriously? But wow, you're actually going to explain this before it happens? You usually wait until we're already in over our heads."

"True enough. But this time, you need to be infoooormed ahead of time. This one could get very tricky. Now then, if you'll excuse me, I have work to do."

Shiraaase stood up, stared at the happy, playing girls for a moment, and then walked away.

It grew quiet.

Only Masato and Mamako were left. The girls' voices were mixed with the sound of the waves, sounding very far away.

"Shiraaase didn't seem like her usual self... She certainly kept her tone light, but you could hear the tension under the jokes. What do you make of it, Mom?"

"......"

"Mom? Are you asleep?"

Mamako's eyes were closed, her expression peaceful. Masato leaned in close, and her eyes fluttered open.

"Eep! So you are awake? You startled me."

"Hee-hee. So sorry. I wanted to join the conversation, but I promised you I would take it easy! So I pretended I was asleep."

"Okay, okay. I get it. Today is your day off. So, uh...if there's something you need to do, make sure you tell me. I'll help any way I can."

"Why, thank you! Then I do have a favor to ask."

"Cool, leave it to me! What should I—yiiikes?!"

Mamako had rolled over and untied her bikini top, exposing her bare back and the overflowing sides of her boobs... Now she was rummaging around underneath the beach chair...

...and handed him some suntan lotion.

"Since today is Mommy's day off, I'm going to make you spoil me, Ma-kun. So will you do the honors? Hee-hee."

"Ha. Ha. Ha. Very funny, Mom."

"Eeeek!"

Helping was one thing—spoiling was another.

Masato squirted a huge glob of thoroughly chilled lotion onto her back.

Meanwhile, in a forest near Materville...

Three of the Four Heavenly Kings were facing Hahako.

"So you're trying to say the master's abandoned us?" Amante said angrily.

"I believe that's what's happened," Hahako replied with a sorrowful nod. "They tried to sink the entire lair in full knowledge that you were still there."

Sorella snorted.

"I doubt thaaat. The master knew we'd be able to get out on our ooown. That's whyyy. They trusted uuus. Clearlyyy."

"But you girls were stuck in a special trap. Do you think you could have escaped that on your own?"

"Erk... W-well..."

"Errrrk... That might have been haaard..."

"There y'all have it! You two are so useless that y'all got kicked out."

"Dammit, Fratello! What the hell is your problem? That's not true!"

Amante tried to grab her, but Fratello easily dodged, blearily glaring back.

"I ain't like you two fools! I sent Mamako Oosuki flying! I got things done! I ain't been cast aside. I still have the master's trust!"

"Do you truly believe that?" asked Hahako. "You were lying unconscious

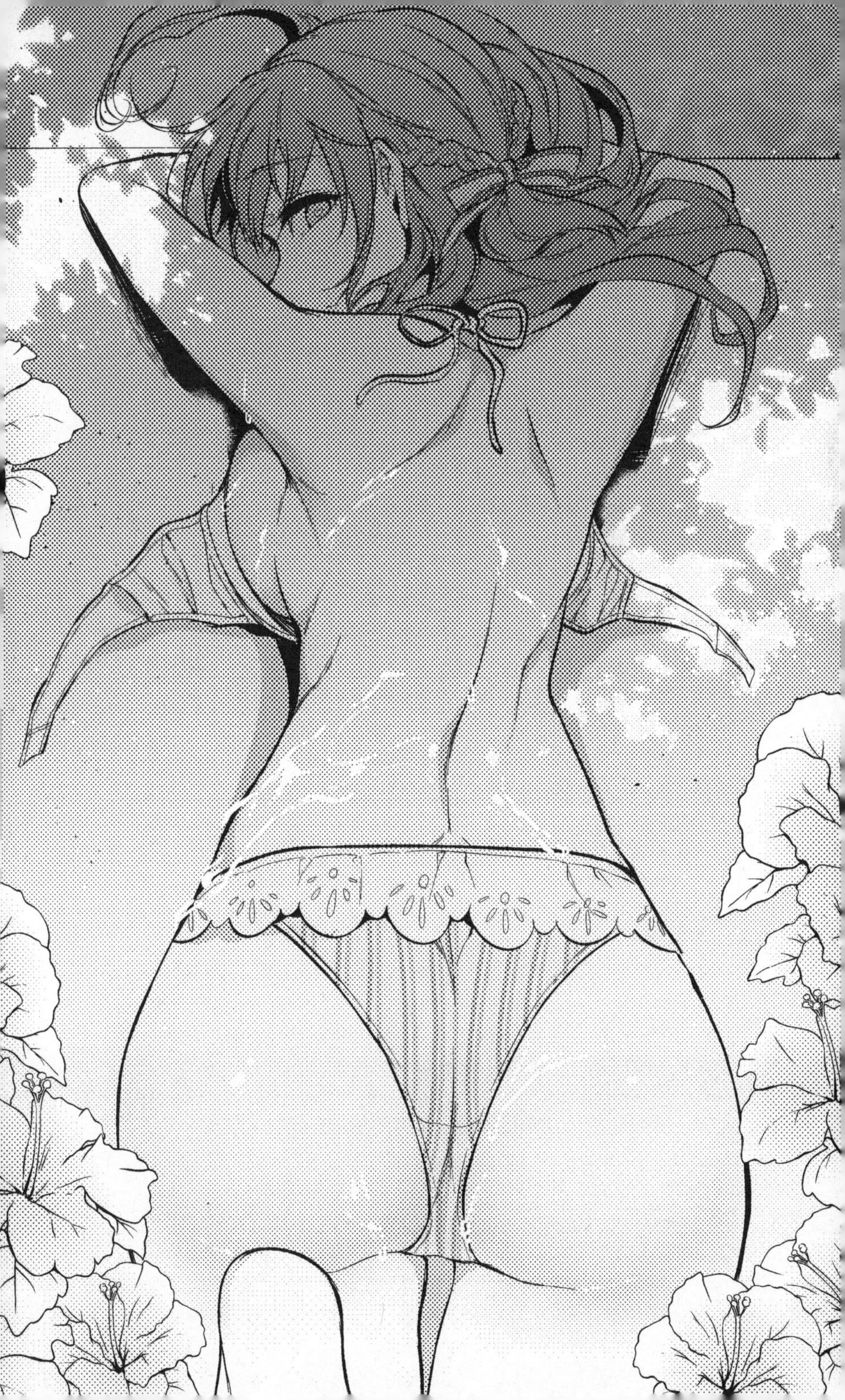

in the lair as it was filling up with water. Do you think you would have survived that?"

"Nope! Fratello just has a specialized skill that works on moms, but her core stats aren't anything special."

"And you lost to Masatoooo, who barely even counts as an enemyyyy. Seriously, Fratello, you're the weakest one heeere. The first candidate for abaaaandonment."

"It's true I lost to that kid. I admit it. But…"

Fratello was clearly furious at being called the weakest one here. She seemed ready to punch Sorella.

Hahako stepped between them.

"Please, don't fight. Deep breaths, everyone! I know this is all very sad, but it's going to be fine."

"Fine? How's that?" Fratello demanded.

"I won't abandon any of you. No matter what. Even if you do something bad, I'll just give you a proper scolding. But I'll still love you. After the scolding, I'll give you a big hug and promise not to let you go. So…"

"We've gotta run before she starts hugging us!"

"Fratelloooo! You take care of the rest, thaaaaanks!"

"Mah?!"

They pushed Fratello into Hahako's open arms.

And then Amante and Sorella hightailed it out of there…or tried to. "Eeeek!" "Auuuuughh?!" Countless white hands rose out of the ground, embracing them securely.

"See here, this is Mommy's embrace. Isn't it lovely? Hee-hee-hee."

"Mah…mah…mahhhhhh! No good, I can't shake her off… Hngggg!"

"Hahako isn't fully a mother yet, so Fratello's power won't work!"

"This is no time to stand around explaining thiiiings! Helloooo?! Masterrrr?! Help uuuus!"

"Master! Master! Are you out there? Please respond!"

"Hnggg… Please, master…if ya don't save our skins, I'm gonna suffocate between her…boobs…"

They called again and again. But no dark swirl appeared. They'd been ghosted.

And one woman gathered the three desperate Heavenly Kings into her embrace.

"They really abandoned you? This master of yours is very naughty."

Hahako sighed and stared up at the sky, her eyes looking somewhere beyond the vast heavens—at the unseen real world—a faint trace of anger in her gaze.

Afterword

Thank you all. This is Inaka.

With your help, we've reached volume seven. This is entirely the product of your constant support. I can't thank you enough.

This volume put the spotlight on the last person you'd expect.

While I'm excited that the time has come, part of me wonders if it isn't a mistake. Although if this were any other series, it would have happened long ago.

The indomitable mother, the children doing their best, new enemies— I hope you enjoyed the story on this uninhabited island.

I received immense help along the way to publication from Iida Pochi., my editor, K, and everyone in editing, publishing, and sales. My heartfelt thanks to all of you.

The manga adaptation by Meicha is being steadily updated. As the original creator, I hope you support the web and print editions! Thank you so much.

Now.

This is a little embarrassing, but I'd like to take this moment to announce something.

They've decided to make an anime of *Do You Love Your Mom and Her Two-Hit Multi-Target Attacks?*!

This was announced at the 2018 Fantasia Bunko Appreciation Festival, which I attended to to pay my respects to all the hardworking producers.

"They're really doing it…"

"They are. We wouldn't go to all this trouble for a prank, would we? (lol)"

Apparently it's real.

Part of me still doesn't believe it. (I'm as wary as a wild thing.)

Or perhaps this is just a dream. You can't rule it out! It seems far more likely.

I can't help it. I was born this way.

I spent too long working part-time jobs and trying to make it as a writer, so the fact that I've won this prize and the prize-winning work is getting animated…I feel like my life has become the plot of a light novel.

At least the dreams I'm having are good ones.

If I may digress: My editor says there are no age limits for light novel authors.

To everyone in my generation who has witnessed the dawn of the light novel boom till the present day: The path lies ever open before you.

As far as anime information goes:

Production is hard at work, and I have a mountain of information I'd love to yell from the hilltops, but there are rules about these things, so I'm limited to what has been officially announced.

I'd love to thank everyone involve with the anime production by name, but like I said above, I can only name people listed on the official site. I wish it were otherwise.

Director: Yoshiaki Iwasaki. Character Designer: Youhei Yaegashi. Series Composition: Deko Akao. Music: Keiji Inai. Animation Production: J. C. Staff.

Thank you all. I'm sure each and every one of you is very busy, but please take care of yourselves!

In the role of Mamako Oosuki: Ai Kayano; Masato Oosuki: Haruki Ishiya.

Ms. Kayano has been involved in the series since the first marketing campaign, so I'm thrilled she'll be reprising the role of Mamako.

Mr. Ishiya…you're ostensibly the main character, but sorry—you won't get many chances to shine. The story you told me about the end of year gift has been an inspiration, though.

I can only hope that everything will proceed smoothly and the result will be a delight.

Everyone working on the anime and everyone looking forward to seeing it, trust that my hands are together in prayer.

Finally:

When I told my mother they were making an anime…

"If it's a hit, think they'll come interview me? I've got loads of photo albums from when you were a child to show them."

Trust that my hands are once again together in prayer that this never comes to pass.

Late fall 2018, Dachima Inaka

NEXT TIME

"To save Ma-kun and his friends, I'll ask Kazuno and Medhimama for help."

The mastermind controlling the Libere Rebellion's Four Heavenly Kings appears! Masato's party is in desperate straits! And they'll be saved not just by Masato's mom…but by *all* the moms?!

The cutting-edge momcom adventure continues with the Mom Party arc!

Do You Love Your Mom and Her Two-Hit Multi-Target Attacks?

VOLUME 8   Contents subject to change.

ON SALE SPRING 2021

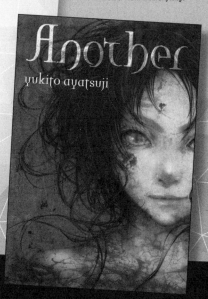